Falling in Love with Emma

by

Pam Binder

Matchmaker Café Series
Book Three

Falling in Love with Emma

Cover Art by *Kristian Norris*

The Wild Rose Press, Inc.
PO Box 708
Adams Basin, NY 14410-0708
Visit us at www.thewildrosepress.com

Publishing History
First Fantasy Rose Edition, 2017
Print ISBN 978-1-5092-1656-7
Digital ISBN 978-1-5092-1657-4

Matchmaker Café Series, Book Three
Published in the United States of America

Emma stood over a batch of cooled sugar cookies and positioned an image of a couple about to kiss over the first in the row. Designing the image and transferring it onto edible sugar sheet paper was the easy part. She'd used the technique before, with her mother's designs. The problem was that she couldn't capture the couple. Something didn't look right. The couple looked like they were fighting instead of on the verge of kissing each other.

Focus, she told herself. *You can do this.*

She anchored her elbows on her work table, holding the piping bag filled with white frosting, and outlined the heart with shell-like swirls.

"Hello, Emma."

Startled by the male voice, she pressed too hard on her pastry tube and a big glob of frosting plopped onto the center of the cookie, completely obliterating the faces of the man and woman.

She'd recognized Björn's voice instantly. One minute she'd been daydreaming about him, and the next he'd appeared as though her thoughts had conjured him out of thin air.

His voice, deep and rich, filled the Boulangerie and flowed toward her like warm caramel. Her heart sped up a notch. Ten notches, if she were being honest. Emma patted her hair into place, feeling the butterflies in her stomach that awakened whenever Björn was around. *Remember, he just wants to be friends.*

Dedication

To my talented and beautiful grandmothers,
Irene Redmond Zollinger and Irene Schultz Pleier,
skilled storytellers who instilled in me
the love of the written word.

A Recipe for a Successful Match

Begin with a mixture of friendship,
Communication and respect.
Add a dash of attraction.
Blend equal parts of commitment,
Trust and honesty,
Now fold in a generous cup of love.

Chapter One

"Emma, did you hear? Björn Erickson is back in town."

Emma Grey gave a quick nod to her grandmother, tucked a rebellious curl behind her ear, and pushed a tray of sugar cookies into the oven. She had heard, in fact; that seemed to be the only thing anyone could talk about.

Located just outside Seattle, Emma's bakery was the heart of a cozy retail shopping area, nicknamed the Village by its residents. She'd awoken this morning confident that today would be like every other.

Then she'd learned that her ex-boyfriend had returned.

Björn had been gone eleven months and twenty-eight days, not that she'd been counting, and in all that time she received not one phone call, post card, or smoke signal from him.

She turned back to her prep station in the kitchen and rolled out more cookie dough. She ran her French pastry shop and her life by a simple philosophy: a place for everything and everything in its place. There was comfort in routine, in knowing your strengths and in knowing your place. She had a safe existence where each day folded into the next. If the consequences meant that you were disconnected from the outside world, that was a small price to pay. She reached for a heart-shaped cookie cutter and attacked the dough she'd prepared. Connections meant risks, and risks resulted in heartbreak, a lesson she'd learned from her mother.

Emma had inherited Emma's Boulangerie the summer she turned eighteen, when her mother had died, and for the past ten years the bakery had remained the same. The French décor was the same, the recipes were the same. Her grandmother took care of the customers, and Emma baked. Her mother used to say there was little room for anything else in life, and Emma agreed.

With its wood cabinets painted meadow green, the kitchen looked like something out of the 1960s, almost a replica of the one used by Julia Child, her mother's favorite chef. There was a six-burner gas commercial range, a refrigerator, and an electric convection wall oven. In tribute to the way Julia Child had arranged her kitchen equipment, copper pots, pans, skillets, and utensils hung from pegboards that covered the walls, and knives were arranged on magnetic strips between the kitchen windows and above the sink. The Julia Child theme spilled out into the pastry shop. Pink-and-black wallpaper depicted images of her beloved Paris. A dozen round, wrought iron tables and chairs, like the ones in outdoor cafés overlooking the Seine River in Paris, were available for customers in the front of the shop. The finishing touch was the letter E embossed on the starched linen tablecloths and napkins.

While she cut the dough into heart shapes, her grandmother, whom everyone called Gigi, was in the restaurant preparing for customers. The windows were closed to keep the shop warm and cozy against the February chill. A fresh pot of coffee was brewing, and the smells of baked bread, vanilla, cinnamon, and chocolate laced the air. Everything was as it had always been: tranquil and orderly. A place for everything and everything in its place.

She reached for one of her recipe books on the shelf above the sink and straightened the small silver-framed photo of a young man. He was cover-model handsome, with a corporate haircut and a well-fitted dark suit. The man's appearance was a stark contrast to Björn's. His family might own the Pisces Fish Market, as well as the Village land and buildings, but Björn was more at home fishing in Alaska than in a boardroom in Seattle's financial district.

She moved the photo more to the center of the shelf. It had accomplished the goal of answering annoying questions regarding her love life. Whenever anyone asked her who she was dating, she'd point to the photo that had come with the frame. She'd explain that the man's name was Jared Montgomery, a name from one of the romance novels she'd read. He was honest and trustworthy. A man who wouldn't leave when things grew complicated.

She adjusted the frame again, knowing full well that she was reversing a projection of her failed relationship with Björn onto her imaginary boyfriend. But imaginary or not, Jared Montgomery served his purpose. When anyone in the Village asked why they'd never met him, she explained that he traveled…a lot.

Jared had bailed her out on more than one occasion. This year she might even send herself flowers on Valentine's Day. Peach-colored roses, perhaps, and a box of dark chocolate truffles.

Emma pressed her hand against her heart. It beat out of control. Thoughts of Björn had that effect on her.

She breathed in deeply the kitchen's rich aromas, trying to bring it back under control. The Bavarian mocha cream cake cooling on a wire rack nearby was one of her favorites: it reminded Emma of her mother. Yes, her life was perfect. She loved her bakery, and the Village was more of a family than a series of retail stores, and thanks to her imaginary boyfriend she avoided a broken heart.

Out in the restaurant she heard the bells over the door chime, announcing their first customers of the day. She recognized the familiar voices.

Dora Jenkins, mother of twin grammar-school-aged girls Caitlin and Catherine, said her children, who dressed only in pink or purple, were both her joy and the reason she lived on coffee, chocolate croissants, and Village gossip.

Mr. Digby followed closely behind Dora and her children. He walked with a limp and reminded Emma of how a Dickens character might look, with his wire-rimmed glasses. Dora had started the rumor that Mr. Digby had a crush on Gigi, a claim Emma hoped was true. Her grandmother deserved a little love in her life.

Emma's grandmother greeted them all with a smile in her voice. She also made sure no one ventured into the kitchen. That was Emma's domain. The only other person allowed in besides Gigi was Daisy, their part-time helper.

The kitchen window slammed open on its hinges, and a cool breeze swirled into the room, and with it the scent Emma always associated with Björn: the salt sea. Outside, a cat wailed and scratched against the door.

Emma wiped her hands on a linen towel and crossed over to the window, half expecting Björn to be waiting outside as he'd done when they were children.

They'd been best friends all through school. He'd even taken her to prom when her own date had stood her up. But all that had been before their lives were turned upside down. Both of their mothers had died within months of each other, and a year ago, Björn's youngest brother, Sven, had drowned in a fishing accident off the coast of Alaska.

But Björn wasn't outside, just her snow-white cat, Ella. A flyer drifted into the room when she opened the door for the cat. It was an advertisement from the new owners in the Village: The Matchmaker Café was having a grand opening ball on Valentine's Day. Parties, especially Valentine's Day parties, weren't for her. She tossed the flyer into the trash as Ella stared up at her and meowed.

"Well, hello to you, too, Ella," Emma said with a smile as she blocked the cat from entering her kitchen. "Have you returned from your adventures so soon? You know you are not allowed in the kitchen. I left you food and…"

In the next instant, smoke billowed out of the oven and smothered the kitchen in a snow-globe haze as Ella meowed again and then retreated to her spot on the back porch, as though she'd accomplished her goal.

Emma rushed over to the oven and yanked out the cookie tray. Heat lit up her fingers. She bit back a scream and dropped the tray. Burned sugar cookies broke over the tile floor as though made of glass.

Her grandmother appeared in the archway that separated the kitchen from the retail area of the bakery. "Are you all right, sweet girl?" Gigi wore the bakery's uniform: crisp white blouse and ankle-length skirt covered in an explosion of wildflowers. Her salt-and-pepper curls framed rosy cheeks and warm brown eyes that always reminded Emma of her mother. "Should we invite Björn over for dinner before he is overwhelmed with invitations? Dora said the Village is all abuzz."

Emma kept her thoughts to herself as she bent down to pick up the mess. The reason she knew he was back, even before Gigi had mentioned it, was that at four o'clock this morning he and his father had made enough noise to wake people for miles around, including the whole Seattle area. Now the village was buzzing like demented bees. Björn was a confirmed bachelor, who besides looking like the actor who played Thor in the Avenger movies was a nice guy. When his older brother Sven died and his father's health declined, Björn had taken the lead in overseeing their fishing fleet in Alaska, while his younger brother, Jorvy, ran the Pisces Fish Market.

"I'm sure Björn is too busy for dinner."

Gigi stared past Emma to the mess on the floor. "Is everything okay in here?"

"Everything's fine," Emma lied as she stood, pushed her aching hand behind her, and reached for a broom to sweep up the broken cookies. Why hadn't she used a hot pad to take out the cookie sheet? She hadn't made such a silly mistake in years, and she hadn't burned anything since she was a child. What was wrong with her?

Gigi seemed to accept Emma's response as she re-entered the bakery, where customers were grouped around tables, sipping coffee and eating pastries. Her voice rose above the hum of conversation as she turned to Mr. Digby. "I've told you before: you can't clean that ridiculous antique rifle on my linen tablecloth."

Emma smiled as she peered at the scene, keeping out of sight. Mr. Digby's eyes twinkled as he pretended he was offended that Gigi had called the replica he'd built of a French blunderbuss rifle ridiculous. Gigi pretended she was upset with him as she brushed an imaginary speck of dust from his shoulder. Mr. Digby had been coming into the bakery every morning for as long as Emma could remember. Emma had asked her grandmother once if she were interested in Mr. Digby romantically, but Gigi had said they were too old for such nonsense and had changed the subject.

The smoke detector clicked, then shrilled overhead. Emma glared at it and whacked it with the blunt end of the broom handle. "Seriously? Now you decide to sound the alarm? My cat has better instincts. Ella tried to warn me that my cookies were burning." She whacked it again for good measure. The detector hushed as though embarrassed.

She headed over to the sink to run cold water over her hand. Like so many things in the bakery, the smoke detector was outdated. It was getting more and more difficult to find replacement parts for her appliances. Money wasn't the issue. Her bakery was doing very well. But Emma had vowed to keep it exactly as it had been the day her mother died in a fatal car crash. The day Emma had been too busy to help with the errands. She turned off the water, dried her hands, and resumed her sugar-cookie project.

She glanced at the Valentine's Day card she'd used to bookmark her cookie page. On it was an image of a couple: a black-and-white silhouette pasted over a heart cut out of pink construction paper. She'd had the card since fourth grade. On the back was the unsigned message, *A Valentine for Emma.* Her secret admirer had never revealed himself, but she'd recognized Björn Erickson's handwriting.

The card had always seemed so grown-up and out of place next to the cartoon and joke-style valentines she'd received in grammar school. She wasn't sure why she felt compelled to recreate the design after all these years, but once she'd begun the challenge, she couldn't let it go.

Emma stood over a batch of cooled sugar cookies and positioned an image of a couple about to kiss over the first in the row. Designing the image and transferring it onto edible sugar sheet paper was the easy part. She'd used the technique before, with her mother's designs. The problem was that she couldn't capture the couple. Something didn't look right. The couple looked like they were fighting instead of on the verge of kissing each other.

Focus, she told herself. *You can do this.*

She anchored her elbows on her work table, holding the piping bag filled with white frosting, and outlined the heart with shell-like swirls.

"Hello, Emma."

Startled by the male voice, she pressed too hard on her pastry tube and a big glob of frosting plopped onto the center of the cookie, completely obliterating the faces of the man and woman.

She'd recognized Björn's voice instantly. One minute she'd been daydreaming about him, and the next he'd appeared as though her thoughts had conjured him out of thin air.

His voice, deep and rich, filled the Boulangerie and

flowed toward her like warm caramel. Her heart sped up a notch. Ten notches, if she were being honest. Emma patted her hair into place, feeling the butterflies in her stomach that awakened whenever Björn was around. *Remember, he just wants to be friends.*

He stood silently on the back porch as though waiting for her to respond, then a Golden Retriever puppy, all big paws and floppy ears, tried to squeeze past him. He blocked the puppy from entering in much the same way Emma had prevented Ella from sneaking into the kitchen.

Emma wiped frosting off her hands, drawn to Björn by the memories they shared from their childhood. She'd forgotten how broad his shoulders were and how his shoulder-length blond hair and blue eyes made her imagine what a Viking warrior might have looked like. Well, maybe she hadn't so much forgotten as pushed the thoughts out of her mind and out of her dreams.

The puppy barked, bringing her back to earth. "You can't bring him into my kitchen," Emma said. "You know the rules."

"Sorry," Björn said, restraining his active puppy with a nod as he attached a leash. "Shark and I are in the stage where we're positioning to see who is the alpha dog in this relationship. I think he's winning," Björn said with a grin as he focused on the burnt cookies in the wastebasket. "Since when do you burn cookies?"

"Everything's under control," she shot back. "And I meant both you and your dog aren't allowed in my kitchen." She winced, knowing how that must have sounded, but he was on the back porch and probably hadn't heard her.

What had gotten into him? He was as much a stickler for rules as she was. Her kitchen was a place of business, not a place for friends to gather.

She thought for a moment that he might have changed his mind about returning to the doorway, then was surprised at the sudden regret she would feel if he didn't come back. She shook it off, as the words her mother had said, on almost a daily basis, repeated in her thoughts. *Build a wall tall and thick enough around your heart, and you won't get hurt.*

But just as she turned back to her project, Björn reentered the kitchen. He moved toward her with a fluid, athletic gait that stalled her heart mid-beat. It was easy to picture him on the high seas, battling storms while fishing for salmon.

She shook her head free of the fantasy and held up her hand. "You can't come in here."

"You keep saying that. I just wanted to see you. It's been a long time." His gaze landed on the Valentine's Day card.

She closed her recipe book and returned it to the shelf. "You left without saying goodbye." Had all the oxygen gone out of the room? If his smile warmed her heart, his expression heated her blood. Just when she had thought she was over him, he'd waltzed back into her life and in mere moments turned it upside down.

He stuffed his hands into his pockets. "It was not a good time for me."

Her stomach knotted. Was it possible he still blamed himself for Sven's boating accident? She lowered her voice, wanting to reach out for him, but held back. "It didn't work out for us as boyfriend and girlfriend, but we're friends. Best friends. Maybe we shouldn't have messed with that relationship." She paused. "I'm always here if you need me."

He reached for the hand she'd burned and turned it over. "You burned your hand. I wish you'd be more careful."

She played along with the shift in conversation. This was classic Björn. He changed the subject when the topic was uncomfortable. She forced a smile. "This from a man who fishes in the ocean, where waves are as tall as New York skyscrapers."

The corner of his mouth twitched into a smile as his large hand wrapped around hers.

It felt like they were holding hands. She cleared her throat. "You named your dog Shark," Emma said, searching for a distraction.

"You named your cat Nutella after your favorite breakfast spread."

"Ella for short," she defended, easing into the comfortable banter they had shared as children.

"I remember that before we'd catch the bus for school in the morning, I'd come over and you'd make me toast with peanut butter and Nutella. I've been thinking about those times a lot lately." He paused, looking at the shelf where she'd placed the recipe book next to the photo. His eyes narrowed. "Who's the guy in the picture?"

Her mouth went dry. She swallowed. "My...my boyfriend. He's a banker." She slipped her hand out of Björn's. "He's very punctual. My hand doesn't hurt anymore. I'm fine. Really."

His eyebrows knitted together as he frowned at the photo. "You are fine, but you still burned your hand.

You don't want a scar."

"I like my scars."

He gazed at her for what seemed like an eternity, as though trying to read her thoughts. "Don't we all."

Chapter Two

"What is that supposed to mean?" Emma said, stepping farther away from Björn. "No one likes scars. That's an absurd comment." The man was infuriating, confusing. One minute she had the impulse to swoon in his arms, and the next she wanted to shove a cream pie in his face.

The bells in the front of the bakery rang out, announcing a new wave of customers. This time the voices weren't familiar and both held a slight Scottish accent. When Emma peered through the archway, she saw that her bakery was crammed with new customers. Although Gigi was handling each order with her usual cheerfulness, the curls on her grandmother's forehead were damp, and there was a slight tremor in her hands as she gave Dora's children complimentary chocolate chip cookies.

"What can I do to help?" Björn said.

"Go catch a fish." Emma said as she rushed to help Gigi with the customers. She berated herself for being swept into Björn's blue-eyed, broad-shouldered net instead of paying attention to how her grandmother was doing.

Besides, she already knew how it would play out with Björn. He'd stay for a few weeks, maybe even a month or two, and she'd fantasize that this time would be different. Then—poof, he'd receive a call that he was needed in Alaska, and off he'd run.

She moved near Gigi and nodded in their wordless code that she'd take over waiting on the women with Scottish accents. The women were at the counter, examining the desserts in the glass case, which ranged from fresh-baked blueberry scones to apple and cherry tarts to chocolate cream puffs.

Despite Emma's suggestion to "go catch a fish," Björn had ignored her to assist Gigi with the line of customers. Her grandmother gave him a grateful nod and a peck on the cheek. Gigi loved Björn, everyone did, which for some reason made Emma even more annoyed at him.

"Excuse me, *mademoiselle*..."

Emma snapped back to help the women at the counter, wondering why they'd greeted her in French. "I'm very sorry. May I help you?"

The woman who'd spoken reminded Emma of how a librarian might look in the nineteenth century. Her hair was pulled back in a bun at the nape of her neck, just clearing the starched white collar of the blouse she wore tucked into a straight black skirt that skimmed her ankles. The other woman was taller and more casually dressed in a cream-colored bulky-knit sweater over slim-fitting slacks, her blonde hair piled haphazardly on top of her head.

"I'm Lady Roselyn." The woman in dark clothes smiled. "And this is my sister, Bridget. We are renovating the old Zollinger barn in the Village and have named our little establishment the Matchmaker Café. Perhaps you've seen our flyers?" When Emma nodded, Lady Roselyn pulled a small notebook from her cloth purse and flipped it open.

Bridget nudged her sister, her voice barely above a whisper. "Did you see her kitchen? It's a replica of Julia Childs'. Don't we have a door that leads…"

Lady Roselyn pinched her sister on the arm. "I noticed, but now is not the time. As I was saying," she said, turning back to Emma. "We are throwing a Valentine's Day Ball in celebration of our grand opening, and everyone in the Village is invited. We've also sent out invitations to the surrounding communities, as well as to our current and former clients. If you're not too busy, would you be interested in supplying a few desserts? I've made a list, but they are only suggestions." Lady Roselyn tore off the sheet of paper and handed it to Emma.

Emma read the desserts listed. Many she already had made in anticipation of the Valentine's Day rush. She, her grandmother, and Daisy would have to work late, but it was doable. "This shouldn't be a problem. When would you need the order?"

"Wonderful news," Lady Roselyn said. "Anytime on the morning of Valentine's will do. Oh, and you can bring your boyfriend," she said, nodding toward Björn.

Emma followed Lady Roselyn's gaze. When Björn caught her staring, Emma kept her gaze focused on his. "We're just friends."

Bridget winked. " 'Just friends' is our specialty."

Chapter Three

After the brief rush, there was a lull in customers, something Emma had learned was a natural occurrence, like the ebb and flow of the tide, or how Björn arrived without warning and disappeared without saying goodbye. She'd settled back into the kitchen to work on the orders from the matchmaker sisters, while Gigi joined Mr. Digby in a cup of coffee. Emma topped her Nutella cheesecake with milk-chocolate flakes and set it next to the other completed orders as she licked sweet frosting off her fingers.

Björn had helped her clean up the cookie mess. So many memories had flooded back at his return, she had to fight to keep from drowning in them.

"Sorry I'm late," Daisy announced, opening the back-porch door. Daisy and her family had moved into the area soon after Emma's mother died, and she and Emma had been as close as sisters ever since. Rain or shine, Daisy wore clothes that reflected her name, no matter the season. She insisted on only happy colors, as she liked to call them, and today was no exception. She wore a meadow-green, pink-flowered blouse with a matching skirt that skimmed her knees, and a raincoat the shade of daffodils.

"Was that Björn I saw leaving the bakery?" Daisy said.

"You know it was."

"My, my, but we're in a mood today. I'd forgotten he has that effect on you. You're like a circus clown with crazy eyes."

"Nice, and he does not affect me like that. It's the day before Valentine's, one of our busiest times of the year. I'm overworked, is all."

Daisy removed her raincoat. "If you say so."

Emma ignored her friend's sarcasm. "Glad that's settled. On to business. We received a large order this morning from the owners of the Matchmaker Café."

"The sisters were here? Cool. I stopped by while they were still unpacking. Their flyers are all over the Village. I'm thinking about going to the party. We should both go."

Emma couldn't believe what she was hearing. Daisy and her cheating ex had gone through a messy divorce, and afterwards she'd vowed never to risk her heart again. That she'd even consider this event shocked Emma. But even if Daisy went, she wouldn't.

Emma shook her head. "A Valentine's Day Ball? Who's the one with crazy eyes now? I plan on having a quiet dinner."

Daisy pointed toward the photo in the silver frame and said innocently, "Oh, do you and Jared have plans?"

"I'm ignoring you."

"Don't be like that," Daisy said. "From what I've learned, the ball isn't the usual if-it-happens-in-Vegas-it-stays-in-Vegas theme party. The sisters offer fantasy-style adventures where you choose the place you want to go."

Emma turned the page in her cookbook to chocolate truffles. "The only place I want to go is

Paris." She started to expand on what she thought of the sisters' ball and holidays that made single people feel lonelier than they had before, but paused. Something in Daisy's expression caught her attention. Daisy might wear cheery clothes, but since her divorce, she'd been as gloomy as a cloudy day. This morning it was as though she'd received an adrenaline shot of sunshine. Emma looked up from her page. "You can't really believe the sisters can recreate a person's fantasy adventure?"

Daisy shrugged as she flipped over the cloth covering the cookies Emma had made before Björn's visit. "I'm not sure what I believe, only that I'm tired of the rut I'm in, and if there's a chance…well, I figure what have I got to lose?"

"I'm not going."

Daisy peered down at the cookies she'd uncovered. "And I'm seriously considering replacing you with a more fun friend. Your aversion to fun runs deeper than mine." Daisy reached over and sampled one of the cookies from the tray. "Yummy. You tried a new recipe. Did the moon turn to butter cream frosting?"

"Ha, ha. Very funny."

Daisy took another bite. "I like nostalgia as much as the next person, but even our regulars have whispered that this place needs a facelift. They want choices for those who are trying to stay away from sugar or are allergic to gluten. It's like the bakery is stuck in the past."

Emma grabbed the tray of cookies and moved it out of Daisy's reach. Emma was aware of their customers' comments. And all valid. But changing even the placement of the tables in the restaurant, let alone the recipes, felt like a betrayal of her mother's memory. "It was a mistake to try something new. I'm not sure…"

A rifle shot blasted through the air. Gigi screamed. Emma and Daisy rushed into the pastry shop. The place was empty except for Mr. Digby and Gigi. Her grandmother sat at the table opposite where Mr. Digby stood, holding his rifle at arm's length. Gigi's face was as pale as the lace collar on her blue sweater. There was a gaping hole in the wall behind her, surrounded by a ring of scorch marks on the wallpaper.

Emma yanked the rifle out of Mr. Digby's trembling hands and set it on the floor, pushing it out of reach with her foot, then rushed over to her grandmother. "Are you hurt?"

Mr. Digby collapsed in a chair and shook his head. "I don't know what went wrong."

Emma cradled Gigi in her arms, searching for injuries. "Are you hurt?" she repeated. "I don't see any blood."

"Don't be too hard on him," Gigi said, but her voice was shaking. "He was showing me how to load the rifle. It takes a lot of skill to…to…" She pressed her hand over her stomach. "I feel queasy."

Emma caught Gigi as she slumped forward. "Daisy," Emma yelled, "call 911."

"They're on their way."

Chapter Four

Hours later, Emma and Gigi returned from the hospital. Thankfully, they had confirmed that Gigi hadn't been shot, and the doctors at the emergency room had checked out Gigi's heart and completed a thorough examination. Their outcome had been to declare Gigi, "Healthy as a horse," and "Fit as a fiddle." Then they had added, "For a woman her age."

The cliché sayings pleased Emma's grandmother, but Emma had heard the underlying message loud and clear. Gigi worked too hard and needed to slow down. Emma knew her grandmother wouldn't slow down without a fight. It would be up to Emma to find a way to convince her.

Emma asked Daisy to continue helping the customers in the bakery, which gave Emma time to broach the subject with her grandmother. She balanced a fresh pot of tea and warm scones on a tray as she opened the door to the enclosed back porch where Gigi rested.

Emma set the tray next to a vase of red roses beside the loveseat where her grandmother sat. Ella was curled up next to Gigi, purring contentedly. Emma was grateful for the peace and quiet. When they had returned from the hospital, there had been a flurry of visitors stopping by to make sure she was okay. Björn had stayed the longest, and Emma tried to push away how much that had meant. Relying on him never ended well.

Dora Jenkins and her twins had made get-well cards, and Mr. Digby had brought the roses along with his heartfelt apology. Emma had overheard him asking Gigi out on a date, with the comment that life was too short, but he had received a polite rejection. Emma thought that was too bad. They made a cute couple. Besides, if Gigi spent time with Mr. Digby it might be the perfect solution to the problem of convincing her to take it easy.

Emma tucked a blanket around Gigi's legs. "The roses Mr. Digby brought were thoughtful."

Gigi flipped through the newspaper she was reading. "Extravagant. Especially right before Valentine's Day. That man has no respect for money."

Emma knew defending Mr. Digby wouldn't do any good when Gigi had dug in her heels. The man owned a thriving clock shop in the Village and was as much of a penny pincher as Gigi. The fact he'd spent so much money on flowers should have sent Gigi a message. Red roses just before Valentine's had to have cost him a small fortune.

Gigi flipped to another page, keeping her head down. "He offered to repair the gaping hole his rifle caused, but the wallpaper is ruined. Your mother ordered it from a French company that is now out of business."

Emma gazed through the kitchen toward the front of the shop. She had already seen the gaping hole in the wall and the scorch marks caused when Mr. Digby's rifle had gone off accidently. The wall would have to be repaired, and she would have to decide to either paint the wall or re-wallpaper the whole room with a new pattern.

She couldn't breathe, then, because it was as though a floodgate had opened. She remembered the day she and her mother had spent wallpapering. Emma had been only six, but her mother had trusted her to spread the paste evenly over the back of the paper. There were Paris-themed prints that came pre-pasted, but her mother had said she doubted Julia Child would approve. Emma had vowed to keep the bakery the same as it was on the day her mother had died. Breaking that vow seemed like a betrayal.

Emma cleared her throat as she turned back to Gigi. "Did you have a good visit with Björn?" Emma asked, trying to sound casual.

"Such a nice boy." Gigi peered over her half glasses toward Emma. "He wanted to know about the man in the fancy silver frame next to your recipe books."

Emma felt a knot form in her stomach. "What did you say?"

"I didn't give your secret away, if that's what you're asking. You should tell him the truth before he finds out on his own." Gigi pushed her glasses up the ridge of her nose and flipped through the newspaper she'd been reading. "I told him he should ask you out."

"Why would you tell him that?" Emma blurted, then clamped her mouth closed. Stay focused, she chided herself. You're supposed to find a way to convince Gigi to slow down, not discuss your love life—or rather, the lack of one. Truth be told, she was pleased with Björn's question and more than curious about his response to Gigi's reply. Was he jealous?

Emma didn't want to sound anxious, so she took her time pouring Gigi a cup of tea and kept her voice neutral. "What did he say?"

"Some nonsense about timing," Gigi said. "Found it." Gigi presented the travel page to Emma. "There's a discount flight to Paris. You should ask Björn to go with you. Life is short. Live a little."

"Okay," Emma said, easing the newspaper out of Gigi's hands as she set it aside. "I think it's time for a nap."

"Don't treat me like a child, young lady." Gigi petted Ella behind the ears, and the cat opened its eyes and leaned its head against Gigi's hand. "I had a brush with death," Gigi said in the same tone Emma used to order baking supplies. "It changes a person. Makes them more outspoken."

Emma had to bite the side of her lip to smother a smile. Gigi had always been the most outspoken person she'd ever met. "Even so, you need to rest."

Gigi tore off a corner of a scone and popped it into her mouth. "Daisy told me there's a lovely Valentine's Day Ball at the new shop in the Village, and that you refused to go. If you're dead set against a relationship with Björn, there are plenty of good men available. My experience made me realize that I'd like at least one grandbaby." Gigi sipped her tea innocently, as though this were the first time she'd brought up the subject of grandchildren.

"Just one? I thought you said you wanted at least four."

"I have no idea what you're talking about. But I'm glad we brought up the topic. You need more in your life than this bakery."

"What about you?" Emma said. "You turned down Mr. Digby's date, and I know you like him."

"You're changing the subject."

Emma sat down next to Gigi. "I'm worried about you. The doctors said you shouldn't work so hard."

Gigi squeezed Emma's hand. "I could say the same about you. But if it means so much to you, I'll consider slowing down a bit."

Emma felt relieved and kissed Gigi on the cheek. "Thank you."

Gigi drew Ella onto her lap. "Now that's settled, what's the real reason you refused to attend the ball?"

"There's too much to do. Plus, Björn and I are just friends."

"The two of you have never been 'just friends.' Blind about your feelings for each other perhaps. Stubborn, most definitely. But never 'just friends.' "

"Björn doesn't want to get married." There. She'd said it. "He told me last year during his brother's funeral."

Gigi stared at Emma in silence. She sat up a little straighter as though she'd come to a decision. "People say a lot of things when they're grieving. I said I'd never date again after your grandfather died. I'll make you a proposition. I'll agree to slow down and go out to dinner with Mr. Digby if you do a couple of things for me. The first is that you must help Daisy take the 'welcome batch' of brownies over to the Matchmaker Café. I intend to sleep in tomorrow. I want to look my best for my hot date with Mr. Digby."

Emma winced at the "hot date" reference. She was happy for Gigi, but she didn't think any granddaughter wanted to hear her grandmother say those exact words.

"That sounds reasonable."

This day had certainly been out of the ordinary. First, she'd burned the cookies, something she hadn't done in a long time. Next, Björn had stopped by unexpectedly and awakened feelings she'd thought buried. A gun had gone off in the bakery, blowing a hole in the wall. Which meant, at the very least, she'd have to repaint. Her grandmother had announced that she was going on a "hot date," and even Daisy, after a messy divorce, was in the mood to date again. Until this morning, the Village had been a quiet, predictable place. Nothing out of the ordinary ever happened. What was next? Mermaids in Lake Sammamish?

Emma rose. "I'll get you a fresh pot of tea."

Gigi's eyes sparkled with mischief as she reached for Emma's hand. "There's one more thing, and this is nonnegotiable. You must agree to attend the Valentine's Day Ball."

Emma smiled, shaking her head slowly. She had a strange feeling she'd been outmaneuvered. "That's blackmail."

Gigi scratched Ella beneath her chin. "Of course, it is, dear. That's what desperate grandmothers do."

Chapter Five

The next morning, a short distance from the Village, along the shores of Lake Sammamish, a velvet, pink dawn cast its magic over the mirror-smooth waters. Standing beside his dad, Björn cast his fishing line over an inlet along the lake's shore.

His dad had fished with his sons since they were old enough to swim. It was one of Björn's fondest memories and one of the things he missed when he was in Alaska. Returning home had been bittersweet. He'd thought he could pick up where he left off, but seeing how much his father had changed over the past year told a different story. It was not only his dad's mental health, it was as though his whole body had shrunk in size.

He cast another glance at the sky and recited the old sailor's proverb, "Red sky at night, sailor's delight. Red sky in morning, sailor take warning." Of late he felt as though his life had been a series of warning signs.

His father pulled the brim of his wool cap farther down his forehead. "Did you ask Emma out on a date, like I asked?" When Björn shook his head, his dad continued, "You know I love you, but you spend too much time examining all the angles of a problem, believing you have all the time in the world to make a decision. Except life has her own agenda, and sometimes she doesn't ask our advice."

Björn reeled in his line and cast it over the lake. The lure dropped and sent ripples over the surface of the water. Björn couldn't agree with his dad more. He'd had a crush on Emma since grammar school, and a year and a half ago, he'd finally gathered enough courage to take their relations to the next level. Then he'd screwed it up.

What did he expect would happen? That she would wait? Forgive him for breaking off their new relationship, and then compounding it by leaving without saying goodbye?

Still in denial, he'd visualized the outcome of their first meeting after a one-year absence differently. He'd bring flowers. She'd leap into his arms. He'd ask her out…

He hadn't worked out the details of where he'd take her or what they would do. He'd figured it would come to him. When he'd knocked on the back door of her bakery, he'd ditched the flowers.

"Emma has a boyfriend. I saw the photo."

His dad squinted as though trying to read Björn's thoughts. "I've no doubt Emma has a boyfriend. That gal's a catch. If you're not careful, you'll miss your chance. Your mother also had a boyfriend. That didn't stop me from courting her."

"I had my chance, but I broke up with her before I left. I was a mess. What you're talking about was a different time and different circumstances."

His father lifted his fishing rod, reeled in the line, arched the rod over his shoulder, and cast it over the lake. "If by 'different' you mean that now men give up when they face a little competition, I agree."

27

"Her boyfriend's a banker and probably keeps normal hours. Home by six, in bed by nine, and out the door and headed to work by seven."

"Sounds boring."

"Emma likes boring."

"Does she? Well, I'm sure you know her better than I do." His dad shifted his weight. "If we catch a trout, your mother will fry it up for our breakfast." He smiled, and his expression was warm with a faraway glow. "I can't think of your mother without thinking of trout."

Björn kept silent as he rubbed his dad's shoulder. His mother had been dead for over ten years. There were times when his father talked about her as though she'd gone shopping or next door to visit friends. Björn was getting used to his father's abrupt changes in topic, and his memory lapses. The doctors said that was to be expected as the dementia grabbed more and more control. Björn was still working through how to respond. For now, he traveled down the same path as his father. It seemed to make his dad happy, and that was all that mattered.

Björn's eyes stung with unshed tears. "Mom makes the best trout breakfasts."

"Damned right she does. Your mother likes those little cookies Emma brings over sometimes, too. What are they called?"

Björn cleared his throat. "Chocolate thumbprints."

"Chocolate thumbprints," his dad repeated. "Your mother likes Emma. Thoughtful girl. She takes good care of her grandmother. Your mother told me this morning that I should tell you to ask Emma to marry you. Made me promise."

"Dad…"

His father shifted his weight again. "A spring wedding. That's the ticket. Your mother and I were married in the spring. I never saw so many flowers in my life, or a prettier bride." He shook his head. "I remember thinking how lucky I was." He heaved a sigh. "After you ask Emma to marry you, don't forget to ask if she wouldn't mind making us a batch of those thumbprint cookies. Your mother would like that."

Björn swiped at his face as he cleared his throat. "I'll ask."

His father's fishing pole arched over the water, pulling him off balance. Björn discarded his own pole as he reached over to help his dad reel in the trout. The fish leapt from the water, struggling to free itself from the hook, then plunged beneath the surface.

His father strained with the effort to reel in the fish. "He's a fighter. Stubborn."

"Sure is. He'll make a fine breakfast."

"Breakfast? Are you daft? You know I won't eat trout now that your mother has passed away. Doesn't seem right, somehow. No, I'm going to catch this monster and toss him back."

His father's memory swings seemed more dramatic than usual this morning. But it didn't matter that his dad wasn't as sharp as he once had been: Björn had never met a finer or better man.

When the trout was close enough to shore, Björn waded into the water, scooped up the fish in his hand-held net, and then handed it to his dad. Björn's dad unhooked the fish and threw it back. The fish splashed into the lake and dove under the water.

With his gaze locked on the trout and the

shimmering water, his dad asked, "What are you going to do about Emma, son?"

It took a few seconds for the words to register. Then it struck him as he watched his father quietly stowing their fishing gear. Björn laughed to himself. His father's memory lapses seemed suspiciously convenient this morning. "Okay, Dad. You win. I'm going to fight for her."

His dad clapped Björn on the shoulder. "Good lad. And don't forget to ask Emma to make me a batch of her chocolate thumbprints."

Chapter Six

Björn set the fishing poles near the entrance of the Pisces Fish Market as his father entered and took the stairs to the apartment above the shop to rest. Björn watched his father, remembering when his dad had been the first up in the morning and the last one to bed. Back then, his energy had seemed endless. Björn shook away the memory as he passed through the shop to the back room.

The indoor market was white walls, chrome counters, and steel sinks. In the front area of the shop, a trough-like table was filled with salmon and crab covered over with crushed ice. The glass counters were filled with a variety of fish and specialty items including swordfish and green pepper on skewers, marinated in his dad's special sauce, next to crab-stuffed mushrooms.

The layout of the backroom was like Emma's kitchen, except hers smelled like cinnamon and chocolate and his smelled like fish guts.

His father was right when it came to Emma. So many missed opportunities, and yesterday was no exception.

Björn headed to the work table, grabbed an apron, and nodded toward Jorvy, who was already at work cleaning fish.

If Björn was to rate his first meeting with Emma

after being gone almost a full year, he'd give himself a D minus. He wasn't sure what he had expected. True, Emma was shy and reserved, so rushing into his arms and slathering him with puppy-dog kisses was not her style. But he had hoped for something a little more welcoming than, "You can't come into my kitchen." What had he expected? He'd seen her boyfriend's picture. Obviously, she'd moved on.

Björn whacked the head off a King Salmon on the center chopping table, while his brother worked opposite him gutting fish.

Björn eyed his brother from across the room. Unlike his dad, Jorvy hadn't changed. While Björn resembled how his father had looked in his prime, Jorvy, although as tall, had a slight build, and his arms and shoulders were covered with colorful tattoos. For now, Björn needed to set his feelings for Emma aside and break the news to his brother that he was leaving the business. He felt the announcement of bad news should be handled in the same way as removing a bandage. There wasn't an up side in going slow: it only dragged out the agony.

"How'd your visit with Emma go?" Jorvy said.

Why couldn't his family let it go where Emma was concerned? Life didn't always end with a happily-ever-after. He sliced off the tail of the fish with one clean blow. "I'm leaving the business."

Jorvy looked over at him from across the table. "Dad predicted you might try something stupid."

"How'd he…"

Jorvy shrugged. "The old man knows a lot more than you think. The big question is why you're telling me this while I'm holding a fish gutting knife in my hand? Ballsy."

"What can I say? I have a death wish."

"Not funny." Jorvy went over to the sink to clean his blade and his hands. "The Pisces is a family-run business. You want a break? Fine. Take a vacation. But Dad and I aren't going to let you quit without a fight."

"I thought you'd like the idea of running the whole business."

"For a smart guy," Jorvy said, turning off the water, "you don't know much. I want my brother back."

Björn rubbed the jagged scar that twisted around his forearm. He'd received the injury that nearly severed his arm the day he'd tried to save Sven. He, his brother, and the crew had been fishing off the coast of Alaska when a freak storm hit. Sven had gone overboard, along with anything not tied down. Björn had dived after his brother into the boiling water filled with shards of broken debris. Only one of them had been pulled out of the water alive.

Björn braced his hands on the table. "I want Sven back too."

"That's not what I meant, and you know it."

"My decision is final."

Jorvy glanced over his shoulder, his voice even. "Just make sure you're doing this for the right reasons. Running away never solved anything."

Björn reached for another salmon but changed his mind. "I've never run away from anything in my life."

Jorvy pushed away from the sink and turned toward Björn. "Our brother's death was an accident. No one blamed you."

Björn slammed his hand on the counter, rattling the knives. "Maybe they should have. And maybe we've given too much to this business. You always said that if you had more time, you'd sail around the world and visit exotic places."

"I was also eight when I said that, and as I remember, my focus was on getting out of homework and a math test." Jorvy pushed away from the sink and headed toward the back door.

"Where're you going?" Björn said.

"You're wrong about everything, and I intend to do something about it."

Chapter Seven

Bridget McBride took a break from polishing the raised wood logo of the Matchmaker Café, a Scottish thistle, to gaze over the cottages that formed a winding path of retail stores. She and her older sister had moved to the Village from Scotland to open the Matchmaker Café, the first café of its kind in the United States. Her younger sister, Fiona, would have loved it here. Some people said their decision to bring the café to the United States was inspired. Others hinted that they were on the run. The truth, as it often is, was somewhere in between.

Bridget's vision blurred. Since leaving the Highlands, she'd had little time to worry if their sister, Fiona, would make it back. Bridget stepped back into the café, closing the door behind her. She slumped against the door. That wasn't true. She couldn't stop thinking about Fiona.

Fiona and her betrothed were still missing. Bridget didn't understand why Fiona had gone back for Liam in the first place. They fought like proverbial cats and dogs, and were petitioning the matchmakers' council to have their betrothal declared null and void. And yet she'd rushed back through time to help him.

Bridget swiped at her eyes, trying to push out of her mind the dangers Fiona must be facing, and concentrated on the present. She understood why her older sister had chosen the Village. It was a picture-worthy setting framed by snow-capped mountains, rolling hills, and crystal-clear water, reminiscent of the Alps and the Scottish Highlands rolled into one. But beneath the most serene landscape and mirror-smooth water lay secrets and hidden desires.

Secrets: the biggest was how their unique matchmaking system worked. Even she wasn't one hundred percent sure.

When it came to matchmaking, Bridget didn't believe in reading manuals or consulting star charts. She and her two sisters trusted their instincts, even though their own love lives were either nonexistent or on rocky ground. Maybe that was the fate of most matchmakers. All their energy was focused on helping others find their soul mates, leaving little time for themselves.

Valentine's Day was in two days, and they'd chosen the holiday for their opening on purpose. Less pressure. Matchmaking couples was more than a job to them: it was the core of who they were, and each one of them had a role. For her part, Bridget wished she'd been born in an age when matchmaking wasn't so complicated…if a time and place like that had ever existed.

"Have you selected our match couple for the grand opening ball?" Lady Roselyn said, joining Bridget on the café's threshold. As usual, her sister was dressed in somber colors that made her look a decade older than her thirty-three years. She also seemed more on edge than normal. In truth, they all were, and it wasn't just because Fiona hadn't returned.

"I thought we had decided against anything

elaborate this year?"

Her sister fingered a charm bracelet on her wrist, one that had belonged to their mother. "Helping couples find their soul mates is as important to us as breathing is to others. It's in our blood. Besides, these days, couples need us more than ever."

Bridget wasn't sure what had changed her sister's mind, but she'd learned from experience that it was better not to ask. She added another rhinestone clip to keep her blonde hair balanced on top of her head. "If you're serious, I have the perfect candidate. Emma Grey. She owns the bakery we visited, and she lives with her grandmother in an apartment over their shop. There is love in everything she bakes, and yet she has refused to welcome it into her own life."

"Well done. And I presume the man you've selected was the one Emma introduced to us as just her friend. Have you selected their adventure?"

Before Bridget could respond, there was a knock on the door, and Lady Roselyn went to answer it.

"I'm still working out the details of Emma and Björn's adventure," Bridget said, more to herself than her sister. "But for it to work, we will need Fiona and Liam."

Chapter Eight

"Where are you going?" Björn said to his brother. "Is this what you meant when you said you were going to do something about my leaving?"

"Not exactly." Jorvy zipped up his duffle bag. "I am, however, taking you up on your suggestion. I've booked a flight to Alaska. Dad wanted to get away. Do something fun. It was either Anchorage or skydiving."

"Let me guess. Dad's been watching the movie *Bucket List* with Morgan Freeman and Jack Nicholson again."

"You got it, and the timing is perfect. It's best if we're out of the way until you sort this out. You have a lot to think about. I sent a message to the Village retail owners that if they have any problems you're their guy until I return."

Björn knew what his brother was doing. With Jorvy away, Björn would be tasked with managing the Village retail shops, making sure their plumbing worked and their lights turned on. But this was no ordinary collection of retail shops. The shop owners cared about each other, sharing the good times and helping in the bad. Did Jorvy believe Björn didn't know how special this place was? But at the end of the day, it was too much togetherness for him to handle. Too many people.

"At least let me drive you and Dad to the airport."

Jorvy slung his duffle bag over his shoulder, then glanced out the window. "No need. Our taxi just arrived. Besides, you're going to have your hands full. The village called an emergency meeting. They were concerned when I emailed that you were in charge until my return. For some reason, they think you plan to paint the cottages gold with purple trim to match the University of Washington Husky football team's colors."

"Who gave them that idea?"

Jorvy grinned. "The meeting is in a few minutes."

"I hate meetings."

Jorvy grinned. "I know. That was a bonus."

Björn stuffed his hands into his jeans pockets. "You're enjoying this."

"You finally said something I agree with."

Chapter Nine

Björn closed the door on the taxi and watched his brother and father drive away. Under the circumstances, Jorvy was right. The only solution was taking their father as far away from the Village as possible. There was no way Björn could explain it to his father without sounding ungrateful.

He heaved a sigh, and headed toward the Village meeting. It was being held in one of the only businesses that wasn't a retail shop: the nonprofit Writer's Cottage. The inside was painted apple green, with white trim on the wood-frame molding, windows, and doors. It resembled a cozy library around the late nineteenth century, complete with antique furniture, bookshelves, and a corner fireplace. People came from all over the Puget Sound area to curl up in one of the leather wingback chairs and spend a quiet afternoon reading, writing their novels, or participating in critique groups. The atmosphere of the cottage was warm and welcoming.

As Björn entered the cottage, however, the expressions of the retail owners were far from warm and welcoming. They were the exact opposite. He recognized most of them, but there were a few new faces. C.C., the woman who planned to open a shop called Sandwich Land, was calling the meeting to order and glanced over at him when he entered. Thankfully,

Emma hadn't arrived, and he hoped that because this was one of her busiest times of the year she'd stay away.

C.C. nodded toward him and raised her voice. "Your brother mentioned you were in charge for the next few weeks. We wanted to make sure you aren't planning any big changes unless we are all consulted first."

Her announcement opened a floodgate of questions, and he spent the next few minutes quieting everyone's fears. The Pisces Fish Market was not only one of the original shops in the Village, his family also owned the land and managed the Village. Björn assured them he wasn't planning on selling while his brother and father were away, nor would he have the retail cottages painted in honor of any football team's colors, including the Seahawks' green and blue.

In between the questions, he made a mental note to wring his brother's neck when he returned.

When everyone seemed appeased, C.C. announced, "We're pleased to learn that although you're leaving, everything will stay the same."

Even as C.C. spoke, Emma burst through the entrance carrying a tray of cherry and meringue pies as well as pink sugar cookies. "What did I miss, and who's leaving?"

C.C. broke away from the others and approached Emma, thanking her for the desserts. "Björn. Jorvy sent the message to me, and I forwarded it to the Village this morning."

Emma blinked a few times as though processing what C.C. had said. In slow motion, Emma turned toward Björn. Her eyes bored into his. He recognized the slow-burn expression in the set of her mouth and the steel glint in her eyes. Emma was only a little bit of a thing, she barely came up to his shoulders, but when she dug in her heels, he'd rather wrestle a shark than Emma Grey when she was upset.

As impossible as it seemed, her expression only darkened. "You neglected to tell me that tidbit yesterday. Would you care to explain?"

"I need to get away, is all."

She stepped closer, holding the tray of desserts between them. She shoved the tray against his chest. "What did your father say?"

"Dad will understand."

"How could someone so smart be so dumb? Have some pie." She lifted the lemon meringue pie from the tray and shoved it into Björn's face. "When you go on vacation, I hope it's someplace far, far away."

Chapter Ten

Returning from helping Bridget distribute flyers for the ball, Lady Roselyn had heard the news that Jorvy had left, leaving Björn in charge, and that Emma, upon learning that Björn intended on leaving for good when his brother returned, had shoved a meringue pie in his face. The event had spread over the Village faster than the onset of a winter storm.

Lady Roselyn chuckled under her breath. "Good for Emma."

Still smiling, she thumbed through the set of keys until she found the one that opened the Matchmaker Café. The key looked so plain beside the others, with only the engraving of their trademark Scottish thistle to distinguish it, and yet in some ways it was the most important of them all. It opened a door to a world of possibilities only dreamed of in the most creative of imaginations.

While she waited for Bridget, she replayed the words that had been buzzing around the Village. In the meeting this morning, Emma had told Björn he should go far, far away, regardless of the fact, which everyone knew, that Emma missed him when he was gone. And then there had been her meeting with Björn's brother, Jorvy. He was a very persistent man and had wanted to hire her to match Emma and Björn. Wherever she had gone today, she'd received a similar request. Well, the matchmakers might have the perfect solution.

She glanced over her shoulder, wondering what was keeping Bridget. The café was enveloped in mist and mystery, exactly as Lady Roselyn had ordered. She'd chosen this city when she'd heard it was nicknamed Seattle Freeze because people kept to themselves and weren't friendly. The sisters' secrets would be safe here, or so she had thought.

Except Seattle wasn't a deep freeze of unfriendly people. It was quite the opposite. To make matters more problematic, those in the Village behaved like small-town America. They asked a lot of questions and were concerned about each other. Good qualities, but that meant she and her sisters would have to be on guard.

They'd achieved the best results when people couldn't peer behind the curtain to learn how things worked. If only their sister, Fiona, were here with them. She was skilled at deflecting questions. But it was more than that. Without her, they felt off balance, missing a necessary part.

And then there was the legend. Supposedly, the doors didn't work properly if there was discord amongst the sisters, or if one of them was missing. Unfortunately, that was only one of the many legends that had clung to the doors with such persistence the matchmaking council had made it, and others like it, a rule. The number one rule was that three sisters must be present if a door was opened.

She rubbed the back of her neck. "Stupid rule," she said under her breath as Bridget jogged into sight through the mist.

"I finished distributing the flyers for the ball," Bridget said as she reached Lady Roselyn and paused to take a breath. "Everyone wants to know what adventures will be available. Without Fiona, we'll have to go old school and match couples without the doors. I'll bring out games, dim the lights, make sure we have a good band and lots of chocolate."

The tension in Lady Roselyn's shoulders eased: she was grateful for Bridget's practical side. "We're matchmakers. We can do this."

"It'll be boring," Bridget said, with a roll of her eyes. She turned toward the mist, growing more serious. "I don't care about the doors. I just want Fiona and Liam to return. Maybe I should go look for them. Did William install the Culloden door?"

Lady Roselyn's tension returned with a vengeance. "You will not try and find them. I forbid it. You need to stay right where you are. The Culloden door is too dangerous. It leads straight onto the battlefield between the Jacobite Scottish rebellion and the English. For the life of me, I don't know why William insists we keep it. We'll give Fiona and Liam a little more time. If they're not back soon, then we'll decide what to do next."

"I still don't understand why Fiona went back for Liam in the first place. He's perfectly capable of taking care of himself."

"As is Fiona. She is a trained warrior." Lady Roselyn kept her head turned from Bridget as she inserted the key in the lock, concerned Bridget might be able to read her expression. She was as worried as Bridget but for a different reason. Fiona racing after Liam was, in part, her fault.

So many times Lady Roselyn had wanted to tell Bridget that. Although she didn't know who was behind the attack on Liam, Fiona, and their clients in Inverness,

Scotland, she'd encouraged Fiona to stay behind with Liam. At the time, she'd felt it was the perfect solution. If ever a couple needed a custom-made matchmaker adventure, it was those two.

She gave the key a jiggle in the lock. Old locks were tricky and required a little nudge, not unlike people.

The lock released.

"Did you know that our former client, Cinderella Charming, C.C. to her friends, was planning on opening a shop here when you signed the lease?" Bridget said, a touch of criticism in her tone.

"An unfortunate coincidence, I'm afraid."

"You don't believe in coincidences. What about our rule of secrecy? Aren't you afraid C.C. will say something about what we do?"

"Would that be such a bad thing?" Lady Roselyn said as she entered the dimly lit café. Curtains were drawn over the windows, allowing only filtered light to peek through. Boxes were stacked like tall buildings, furniture piled in corners, waiting placement next to doors yet to be installed. The good news was that the work needed to prepare for their grand opening would prevent her from thinking too much.

Even so, it was as though she were drowning in secrets and rules.

A light pulsated from the far side of the room, drawing her attention. A door had opened. Light spilled out, spreading over the floor in a golden path. Lady Roselyn dropped her set of keys as Bridget gasped and clapped her hand over her mouth to stifle a scream.

Silhouetted in the entrance of the Culloden door were Fiona and Liam, locked in each other's arms in a kiss so passionate Lady Roselyn felt her face heat in a blush.

Chapter Eleven

"Are you ready?" Daisy said, as she pulled two cherry pies from the oven and set them on the counter to cool.

Emma arranged the frosted brownies on a ribbon plate and nodded absently. "Just so we're clear. We're going to drop off the welcome gift and come right back," Emma said. "I still have orders to complete."

Daisy shrugged on her raincoat and opened the door. "You work too hard. If you ask me, Gigi's not the only one around here who should slow down. Oh, and she texted me to remind you that you promised to attend the ball."

Emma wound a green scarf around her neck, pulled on her coat, and then reached for the plate of brownies. She was thankful the rain was taking a momentary break. The air still felt soaked and heavy, while the clouds overhead debated whether to allow a sun break. "Gigi texted you? I didn't even know she knew how."

Daisy made a slight bow as Emma breezed through to the open door and headed down the winding brick path toward the Matchmaker Café. "Most people are more complex than we give them credit for."

Emma nodded to one of the shopkeepers she passed. "You're becoming a philosopher."

"I know." Daisy grinned. "I think it's all the excitement about meeting someone new."

"Just so we're clear: I agreed to go: I did not agree to meeting a stranger."

"Speak for yourself."

Except Daisy made the prospect of the ball sound like so much fun that for a moment Emma was drawn into the conversation on what to wear and how to style her hair. Daisy chatted away beside her, carrying on about the mystery shop and its grand opening ball and whether she'd wear her red dress or the black one with the beaded belt.

The buzz of power tools filling the air as they reached their destination brought Emma back down to earth.

The newly renovated shop was on the outskirts of the Village and had been abandoned for years. Twinkling lights that framed the buildings and weaved around trees and pathways doubled in number as they reached the new shop's porch. Two large moving vans were parked nearby as a parade of workers carried furniture, crates, and boxes inside.

A distinguished-looking older man descended the café's stairway at the entrance. He had a salt-and-pepper beard and wore a tweed jacket. He tapped his wool cap in greeting. "A fine morning to you," he said in a thick Scottish brogue, handing Emma a flyer. It was a copy of the ones that had blanketed the village like confetti on New Year's Eve. "The name's William."

Without another word, he adjusted the stack of flyers under his arm, tapped his cap again, and headed in the direction of the other shops.

Daisy turned to gaze in William's direction. "I predict this will be the best party we've ever attended."

"What happened to you? I thought you hated parties."

"I know. Right? I've been wondering the same thing." Daisy stepped aside as one of the men from the moving vans carried a large crate around to the back entrance. When he'd walked out of range, she leaned in closer to Emma. "All I know is that I woke up this morning and, despite the rain, it felt like the sun had never been brighter. I called my brother and told him he worked too hard and should start dating again, and then I vowed to stop wasting any more time thinking about my cheating ex. Does that make sense?"

In a weird, unexplainable way, it did. Emma gave her friend's hand a squeeze. Daisy deserved a little happiness in her life, and as odd as it sounded, the closer Emma drew to the entrance to the café, the more excited she became, as though something extraordinary was about to happen.

The first thing she noticed was that the old barn-red door was gone, replaced by one made from solid oak and polished to a high gloss, so mirror smooth she could see her reflection. In the center of the wood was a raised image of a Scottish thistle.

Emma took a breath and knocked.

The door opened a few inches, and a young woman in her twenties with a blonde ponytail and black rimmed glasses appeared.

She held out her hand. "My name's Fiona." Her smile lit up her delicate features as she glanced toward Emma's welcome gift. "Someone brought us brownies," she shouted over her shoulder. Behind her, the activity pulsated in vibrant purple, red, and pink lights, reminding Emma of a giant kaleidoscope.

Normally, when she brought a welcome gift the person invited her in for a visit. Instead the woman blocked the entrance like a guard at the gates of a secret kingdom.

"Well, I can see that you're busy," Emma said, turning to leave.

"Wait. Where are my manners?" Fiona said, opening the door wider. "Would you like to come inside?"

Chapter Twelve

The inside of the Matchmaker Café vibrated with activity. A maze of boxes containing china and silverware had been unpacked and their contents arranged in groupings over the floor. Wingback chairs, couches, as well as ladderback wooden chairs, were positioned over oriental carpets, and lamps with red velvet shades were arranged on tables. It looked as Emma expected a shop would look on moving-in day, but the notion of getting everything ready in time for a party seemed an impossible task.

The only odd detail was that instead of wood paneling or wallpaper or even paint, the owners had chosen to cover the walls corner to corner with doors.

The door closest to Emma was made of oak and stained a deep walnut brown. There were raised images of a forest carved into the wood. Deer hid behind bushes, and squirrels and rabbits perched on fallen tree trunks. An owl sat on a low-hanging branch, while a winged fairy hovered in the sky as though guarding her domain. It was the most unique carving she'd ever seen. The images seemed so lifelike.

Feeling compelled, Emma reached for the brass doorknob.

Fiona gave a nervous laugh and pulled Emma away. "That door just arrived with a new shipment. We haven't completed the door charm yet."

"Charm?" Emma said, "As in a spell?"

Fiona scrunched her eyebrows together. "Did I say 'charm'? What I meant was we haven't changed the locks."

"Locks and charms are not the same thing," Daisy said under her breath to Emma.

Emma ran her hand over a plain blue door next to the one she'd tried to open, while Fiona was pulled away by one of the workman. The door looked oddly familiar.

Emma leaned toward Daisy. "I agree, but maybe it's her code for lock. When you and I have a disagreement, instead of saying we'll talk it over, we say we'll bake." Emma paused, examining the blue door more closely. "You're going to think this is strange, but I swear I've seen a door that looks like this one before."

"Duh! It's in your mother's photo album of the pictures she took when she visited Julia Child's exhibit at the Smithsonian. What are those numbers printed in the center? An address?"

Emma traced her fingers over the numbers and shook her head. "Nineteen hundred and seventy is the year Julia Child's French cooking book was first published in the United States."

"You are very observant," Fiona said, rejoining Emma and Daisy. "Bridget mentioned that you decorated your bakery with a Paris theme. We found this door on the property in France used by Julia Child and her husband. I'm sure it's my imagination, but late at night, I'm convinced I can hear pots and pans rattling and smell Julia's famous Beef Bourguignon."

"Emma loves everything French," Daisy said with

a smile.

Emma nodded as a memory tugged at her heart. Her mother teaching her how to select cheese or loaves of baguettes or eating warm chocolate croissants while they strolled like Parisians along the Seine River's pedestrian walkway. If she ever returned, would retracing her steps be too painful, or instead would she feel closer to her mother? Now where had those last thoughts come from?

She dredged up the response she knew people gave when they told themselves they'd never have the time or had no intention of going in the first place. "Europe is too expensive right now. Daisy, we should leave." Emma turned to Fiona. "Thank you for showing us around. I know your party will be a success."

"Or we could stay and help," Daisy added with a wide-eyed hopeful stare as she pinched Emma on the arm.

Emma didn't mind the pinch. Her friend was right. Besides, Daisy's mood was infectious. Or maybe it was this place. Despite the disorder caused by all the unpacking and parade of deliveries, it felt as though the café extended its arms and embraced her in a warm hug.

She nodded. "Yes. We'd both like to help. If you need us."

Fiona's smile lit up her face. "How generous. My sisters and I knew we were right about you two. And because you were so sweet to offer, you all may choose from our selection of romantic fantasies at the ball. We offer games, competitions, or journeys to places you've always dreamed of visiting."

Emma leaned toward Daisy and whispered, "Do

you know what she's talking about?"
        "Didn't you read the flyer?"

Chapter Thirteen

Lady Roselyn counted out the silver linen napkins edged with embroidered red hearts, lost track of the number, and recounted as she watched Fiona direct Emma and Daisy over to a stack of boxes. "Has our sister lost her mind?" Lady Roselyn said to Bridget. "She's asked perfect strangers to help us prepare for our grand opening."

"I think it is a great idea. Emma and Daisy will be a big help, and it makes us look like we want to be part of the Village."

"You're missing the point. We left Scotland in such a hurry that I can't be sure what's in the boxes."

Bridget looped her arm through Lady Roselyn's. "Don't worry. I'm pretty sure our great-grandmother's teacup collection won't animate and start dancing around the room as though they were in a scene from the movie *Beauty and the Beast*."

"That's not funny, and you know what I mean."

Bridget nodded. "Okay, I admit it's not like our sister to ask strangers for help. She's been acting oddly ever since she returned. But we have a lot to do in a short amount of time, and maybe she thought she was helping. Are there any boxes we shouldn't open?"

"Helping or not, the last thing we need is for our guests to start asking questions." Lady Roselyn gave up on counting out napkins and tossed them in the center of the long table. "I think I attached red tape on our file boxes with our records and blue tape on the ones containing travel packages. Or was it the other way around? The ones I'm worried about are the boxes with our pictures. I can't remember how they were labeled."

Bridget gave her sister a hug. "No worries. You keep setting the tables, and I'll oversee the unpacking. And I'll send Fiona over to help you."

Lady Roselyn smiled a thank-you as Bridget rushed away, leaving her to finish setting the table. Soon the guests would arrive. She'd wanted this event to be uncomplicated. That had been wishful thinking. There was no such thing where she and her sisters were concerned. Sometimes she wondered what it would be like if they hadn't inherited their gifts from their mother and grandmother. Their lives wouldn't be as exciting, that was for sure. But would they have been happier?

"I've been doing this for too long," she said with a deep sigh, as though speaking the words aloud would give her answers.

She knew her sisters considered her to be in charge, the person with the final word. She'd never been the fun one. She was the serious, responsible one. Maybe it was because she was the only one who'd been married, and the one who'd looked after them after their mother had died.

She rolled her shoulders to ease the stress, but the burden remained and then increased when Fiona approached.

"The grand opening will be a colossal failure," Fiona said under her breath as she settled down to polish the silver. "There's not enough time."

Lady Roselyn eyed her youngest sister, worrying

about her out-of-character comment. It wasn't like her to be so negative. Fiona was the eternal romantic, and her gift was that she could choose a person's soul mate. But of late, she'd seemed like she was going through the motions. She was distant, as though lost in another time and place. Lady Roselyn had first noticed the shift in Fiona at Stirling Castle when they had matched Logan and Irene. Over Christmas Eve, Fiona had been missing most of the time, and Lady Roselyn suspected she'd met someone. Then on New Year's Eve Fiona and Liam had fought like cats and dogs. Lady Roselyn pushed those incidents out of her mind as an overreaction when she'd witnessed the passionate kiss between Fiona and Liam.

But something wasn't right.

She rested her hand on Fiona's shoulder and gave it a gentle squeeze. "Is there something you'd like to discuss? We haven't had a chance to talk since your return."

Fiona nodded toward Bridget. She was directing one of the moving men on where to install a door. "Our family has used this company for generations, and I was sure I sensed a spark between Bridget and the owner, Mac McDonald, but they treat each other like strangers."

Lady Roselyn followed her sister's gaze, only half focusing on Bridget and Mac. She didn't know if Fiona was avoiding her question or honestly concerned with Bridget's love life. The three sisters were skilled matchmakers. They were also skilled at keeping secrets.

"We advise our clients that playing matchmaker to a friend or relative doesn't always work and might backfire. We should take our own advice."

Fiona glanced over at Lady Roselyn and smiled. "Speaking of meddling in a relative's love life, how *did* you manage to orchestrate the trouble in Scotland over New Year's? It felt very real."

Lady Roselyn laughed softly, pleased Fiona had seen through the ruse. "I had nothing to do with the attack on our guests by Bonnie Prince Charlie's Jacobites, or what happened with the door, but like a true matchmaker, I took advantage of the situation." She massaged Fiona's shoulders, surprised at how tense her sister was. "You know as well as I do that a person must be open to the possibility of love. Bridget isn't ready. Give her time."

"I'm worried I'm losing my matchmaking gift," Fiona admitted.

Lady Roselyn drew back. That Fiona could voice the one thing they feared most took her off guard. She said the only thing she could. "That's impossible."

"Is it?"

"Listen to me. We can choose to use our gifts or ignore them, and from time to time it might seem our gifts are on the fritz, but they never go away completely. You must trust me."

"You're right. I guess I'm just tired."

Lady Roselyn fought back a wave of apprehension. Fiona seldom agreed with her and never admitted to being tired. She bit back a flood of questions and resorted to safe ground. "We can host this party in our sleep. You know as well as I do that once we schedule a matchmaking event, we can't cancel. We'd lose our license, and we're already on shaky ground. This event will be easy. Tomorrow is Valentine's Day. In a few hours, our café will be filled with people open to love."

Fiona reached for the same fork she'd polished a few minutes ago, and polished it again. "I'm not interested in those who have committed to each other already," Fiona said. "I want to help those who are afraid to risk their hearts."

Lady Roselyn held back a response, watching her sister. Fiona's comments, although valid, sounded personal, as though she were speaking about her own inner turmoil. To test her theory, she said, "If you're worried about Emma and Björn, the timing might not be right for them."

"I know," Fiona said. "Matchmaking is what we do. We help people get out of their own way. We help them find love. The ever-after kind. The kind where committing isn't scary, it's exciting. However, we never think of the consequences to ourselves. We witness people in love and can't help wanting it for ourselves."

"I want that for you too," Lady Roselyn said. "You and Liam…"

Fiona shook her head. "We joke about my sprinkling magic matchmaking dust over our couples. Well, I think a generous amount dumped all over me." She turned and gave Lady Roselyn a half-hearted smile. "I'm in love with two men."

Chapter Fourteen

The morning of Valentine's Day, Björn arrived at his store early. His dog shot out of the truck and raced toward the woods in search of squirrels. It was that time in the Northwest somewhere between the dark shades of night and bright promise of day. His father had always said that, at this time of the morning, night and day arm-wrestled to see who would win. It had also rained the night before and the walkways and buildings had that scrubbed-face appearance.

Björn wasn't the only early riser. The smells of sweet bread baking drifted from both Emma's bakery and the new sandwich shop, making his stomach grumble. When he was in high school he would sneak over to Emma's and be treated with fresh breakfast rolls straight from the oven.

Dora, the owner of the yoga shop, waved at him as she unlocked her door. Her twin girls played tag along the walkway. Old memories of these people flooded back. The yoga instructor had once been a programmer for a tech company in Seattle, but burnout had made her reevaluate her life. The children playing tag were age six, or were they closer to eight now? He thought he remembered their names were Caitlin and Catherine.

His dog returned from the chase and settled at the entrance to the Pisces Fish Market. If he was reading his dog's expression correctly, Shark was seriously miffed. Most dogs didn't care whether they caught a squirrel. His golden retriever wasn't like most dogs. He only chased something he wanted to catch.

Björn leaned down to remove a few twigs from Shark's long hair. "I have a feeling this is going to be a long day." The puppy barked and wiggled in response, forcing a smile from Björn.

Björn unlocked the door, thinking he could not feel worse, and then changed his mind. The shop was dark, cold, and empty. His brother had always made it in before him. Coffee would be brewing, and their dad would be seated by the window, reading the newspaper and swearing about something he'd read on the editorial page.

Björn flicked on the lights, then wished he'd stayed in the dark. The glass counters were bare. All the fish and specialty items were in the walk-in freezer, so the display cases were also empty. He had a lot to do before the store opened. His dog barked from outside as though to snap Björn out of his dark thoughts.

"You're right. These cases aren't going to stock themselves." He chuckled. Those were the exact words his father would say to him and his brothers when he woke them in the morning for their chores.

Every morning before they caught the bus for school, the job assigned to Björn and his brothers was to make sure all the display cases were filled, while their parents prepared the specialty items for the day. Sometimes it was clam chowder, sometimes fish stew, and other times maybe crab-stuffed halibut or some other customer favorite.

Shark gave a soft bark as one of Dora's children skipped to the entrance, bent down, and patted the dog's head. It responded by licking the girl's rosy cheeks.

She giggled and looked over at Björn and stretched out her hand, holding a large Valentine's Day heart. "It's from Emma."

She never forgot this day. The note on the back said that she was sorry she'd plastered his face with pie and she wished him a Happy Valentine's Day. On the surface, the message was nice. Maybe that's what bugged him so much. It was the type of message friends sent each other.

What did he expect? If he was being honest, he'd expected to breeze back into her life as though nothing had happened. He'd do what he normally did—stay for a while and then take off for Alaska—and the cycle would begin all over again.

But the look on her face when he first saw her this time told of a different story outcome. She was tired of waiting.

"Thank you, Caitlin," he managed.

She scrunched up her nose. "You keep forgetting." She let out a dramatic sigh. "I'm Catherine. My sister wears pink. I wear purple."

"I'll try to remember."

His response seemed to satisfy Catherine. She gave Shark a hug around his neck and ran back to her mother's studio.

He leaned against the door jamb, watching the two girls scamper away. Shark nuzzled against his leg, and he reached down to pet the dog behind its ear. "You're right. I'm such an idiot."

Chapter Fifteen

Ready or not, the morning of Valentine's Day had arrived. Lady Roselyn had set the breakfast table carefully, in their private apartment over the café. She wanted everything to be perfect when she made the announcement to her sisters. She'd only had a few hours of sleep last night: learning that Fiona was in love with two men had rattled her more than she had first wanted to admit. But she had decided to paraphrase Scarlett O'Hara's last comment in the movie *Gone With The Wind*, Fiona being in love with two men was a problem for another day.

"Concentrate on one issue at a time" had always been her mother's advice. First, she'd deal with what she was going to say to her sisters this morning, and then together they'd strategize the best way to get through tonight's ball.

She glanced over the display of food on the table. She could have ordered the desserts from Emma or bought them at one of the local stores in the area, but it wouldn't have been the same. Plus, she knew Emma had a lot on her mind right now. Björn did, as well. It was a common trait with people these days. Fearing rejection, Emma and Björn danced around the topic of commitment, each afraid of making the first move. A safer bet was independence, even if loneliness was the prize.

This dilemma was always interesting to Lady Roselyn. To most people, the decision seemed easy. But if it were easy, matchmakers would be out of a job. This was where the sisters did their best work. They liked giving couples opportunities to explore the depths of their feelings for one another, and she had just the adventure designed for Emma and Björn.

But that would have to wait. Right now, she had something she needed to tell her sisters. She had set the table using their mother's best china: the plates with the blue flowers that always reminded her of Scotland. She'd also laid out their grandmother's Francis I sterling silverware and matching tea set and the white lace napkins she'd bought in Ireland. She may have gone a little overboard, but what she was going to tell her sisters was something they'd never faced before.

Displayed on the table were some of her sisters' favorite desserts—Bridget's cherry-fudge cake and Fiona's raspberry-orange turnovers. Lady Roselyn had also baked lemon cheesecake, and a Valentine strudel, in honor of the ball, and made a batch of almond fudge and one of chocolate sponge candy.

"What's all this?" Bridget stood in the arched entrance of the dining room, rubbing sleep from her eyes.

"We have a busy day ahead of us, and I thought it would be nice to sit down and enjoy some time together before we got started." Lady Roselyn reached for the teapot, needing something to occupy her hands. What she wanted to do was to wring them and start wailing like a crazy person. Just breathe, she said to herself.

Bridget circled the table before sitting in the chair closest to the windows. "Desserts for breakfast? Our mother baked desserts for our birthdays or when she had news to share. What's wrong?"

"Why does anything have to be wrong?" Lady Roselyn filled her teacup and offered to fill Bridget's. "And I never understood why there seems to be such a double standard. People think nothing of eating cinnamon rolls and donuts dripping with frosting, or crepes with lingonberries and cardamom cream for breakfast, but those same people consider a lovely cheesecake inappropriate first thing in the morning."

Bridget shook out the linen napkin and placed it on her lap. "I get it. You'll tell me when Fiona arrives. Have we decided where we should send Emma and Björn?"

"I have indeed. I'll fill you in after we eat. After breakfast, I want you and Fiona to pay Emma a visit at the bakery. I'll give you a list of the costumes and accessories to take with you. You can tell her it's a thank-you for her help setting up the café. William will supply Björn with what he will need to wear."

"What about Daisy?" Bridget said.

Raising her teacup to her lips, Lady Roselyn smiled and took a sip. "You're quite right. Take over a selection of gowns for her as well. I have the perfect surprise in mind."

"Why are we having desserts for breakfast?" Fiona yawned as she shuffled into the room, holding a travel mug filled with coffee. "What happened?"

"I asked the same thing"—Bridget winked—"but our sister is being mysterious. It's my theory that she's buttering us up before she breaks the news."

"We have access to Julia Child's kitchen," Lady Roselyn said. "It seems a waste not to use it. And

Fiona, where did you get the coffee? I made a fresh pot of tea."

Fiona sat down next to Bridget, sipping her drink. "I wanted a latté. There's a great coffee shop in the Village, and one of the baristas looks like that actor from the TV show *Arrow*. I can't remember his name."

His name is Stephen Amell," Lady Roselyn said as she yanked her napkin off the table and spread it over her lap. "Don't you think you have enough men in your life?"

Bridget glanced between Fiona and Lady Roselyn. "What am I missing?"

"Nothing," Fiona and Lady Roselyn said at the same time.

"Okay, don't tell me. I'll find out for myself. On the topic of men," Bridget said, as she cut a slice of the cherry-fudge cake and placed a generous wedge on her plate, "are you and William finally announcing your engagement? Is that the reason for all the desserts?"

"You know the council forbids us to remarry, and besides, William and I are just friends."

"Friends with benefits," Fiona said with a wink.

"That's absurd." Lady Roselyn's teacup trembled as she took a sip. The direction of the questioning made her uncomfortable. She couldn't entertain the idea of marrying again, and it had nothing to do with the rules of the matchmaker council. "Can't I do something for my beloved sisters without you thinking I have an alternate motive?"

Fiona and Bridget turned toward each other and mouthed, "*Beloved sisters*?"

Fiona stabbed one of the raspberry turnovers with a fork. "Did you and William break up?"

Lady Roselyn lifted her chin. "We are not children. We did not break up… That is we were never… I mean we…"

Bridget leaned forward. "Fiona and I were only teasing. But I get dibs on being your maid-of-honor when the two of you do marry. So now that we ruled out you and William as the reason for this dessert spread, what is really going on?"

"Andrew Campbell arrives soon."

Bridget sat back in her chair. "Whoa, no wonder you baked. Isn't he a member of the matchmaker council?"

Lady Roselyn nodded, keeping her voice calm. "He was installed on the council when his father died last fall."

"They're sending Andrew to spy on us," Fiona added.

"We can't know that for sure." Lady Roselyn jabbed the pastry on her plate with a fork, but Fiona had voiced her worst fear. The council had always left them alone, trusting in their judgment. She didn't like the idea of Andrew's visit. She didn't like it one bit. "The council said it was part of some new policy."

"You don't believe that any more than we do," Bridget said.

"There's more. The council said Andrew will work alongside Liam on tonight's adventure."

"Liam will hate that arrangement." Fiona curled her legs under her as she sipped her latté. "But I have the perfect adventure we can send this Andrew person on. Do you think William has installed the door that leads to the dungeons in the Tower of London?" Fiona said it in a voice as sweet as sugar frosting.

Lady Roselyn frowned as the teacup rattled in her hands. "Promise me that under no circumstances will you do anything that dangerous."

Bridget took the cup from Lady Roselyn. "Fiona is only joking."

Lady Roselyn eyed Fiona as she sat calmly drinking her latté. "I doubt that seriously."

Chapter Sixteen

Back at the bakery, Emma finished frosting a seven-layer chocolate cake with raspberry filling, trying in vain to ignore as Daisy continued singing a never-ending list of love songs. She had been that way ever since they'd returned from the Matchmaker Café the day before.

Emma had planned to leave the café right after they'd delivered the welcome brownies, but when the time came she'd surprised herself by agreeing to stay and help. She must be losing her mind.

Helping set up for the party had been fun. Emma had even managed to read the outlandish claims the sisters had made in their flyer. In addition to games and competitions held in the café, behind the doors were reenactments of places and events. Fiona hadn't allowed Emma to peek, but if the claims were true, no wonder the sisters expected a crowd.

But why couldn't Daisy have wanted to go to a normal Valentine's Day party? One with loud music and floor-to-ceiling chocolate. Fiona also had wanted to know Emma's and Daisy's fantasies of the perfect mate. Emma had expected Fiona to ask the usual, such as. "Do you like tall, dark, and handsome, or someone with a brain, or both?" Instead, she'd opened a book of legendary heroes: Superman; Batman; Spiderman.

When Daisy zeroed in on the Thor character and

then wiggled her eyebrows, Emma thought she'd lose it for real. Everyone in the Village seemed bent on making the comparison between the Norse god and Björn Erickson.

Daisy stopped singing Beyoncé's "Crazy in Love" as she rushed over and opened the door. "They're here!"

In a matter of seconds, Bridget and Fiona swept into the bakery, carrying armfuls of dresses and accessories.

"This really isn't necessary." Emma might as well have been speaking to the seven-layer chocolate cake.

The evening gowns were silk confections, from the palest pinks to the most vibrant reds to various other colors of the rainbow. Each glittered with crystals, beads, or silver and gold threads. In only a few moments the dresses had been hung up, shoes and accessories arranged, and a satchel containing makeup opened.

"When this night is over," Fiona said, "you and Daisy will see yourselves the way others see you."

Bridget nodded, holding a crystal necklace against a rose-pink strapless gown. "Sometimes all a person needs is a gentle nudge in the right direction."

The walls felt like they were closing in. Emma stepped back, holding up her hands as though to fend off an army. She knew a part of her was curious, excited even, at what they could do to make her feel beautiful. The other part was terrified. You only saw the makeovers that worked. What if she was not that person? What if she still looked her boring old self? "What about Gigi? I can't leave her alone."

Daisy reached for a blue dress, holding it up so she

could look at it in the mirror. "Nice try. You know very well that your grandmother is going on her hot date tonight with Mr. Digby. Do you think this shade of blue is right against my skin, or should I choose something in another color?"

"It's not a hot date: they're just friends. What if she needs me?"

"Gigi can take care of herself. And you are running out of excuses. The bakery is closed. I helped you put the sign up myself. Your only job is to sit still and let Fiona and Bridget work their magic. You heard what Bridget said: You just need a gentle nudge."

"This feels like a shove."

Daisy shrugged and reached for a gold dress that glittered like it was on fire. "Stop mincing words. You're going."

"You're very bossy."

"I've learned from the best."

Chapter Seventeen

A few hours later, the Matchmaker Café had been transformed into a fantasy wonderland that shined as though the walls had been dusted with crushed rubies. Crystal chandeliers hung from the ceiling, while a band played love songs in the background. It looked like the café had tripled in size. In the center of the room was a five-tiered chocolate fountain surrounded by Valentine-themed desserts. People crowded into the café, dressed in anything from simple evening wear to elaborate costumes.

Emma had chosen a floor-length red sheath and had to admit that she felt like Cinderella at the ball. She had insisted that her hair still be pulled back but had made the concession of allowing Bridget to arrange curls to frame her face. When they had asked her what fantasy reenactment she'd like to experience, she had been at a loss.

Daisy had always wanted to be a professional dancer and had chosen the dance competition. She was required to dance one full dance with each candidate before making her selection. Her first dance partner had executed the dance steps flawlessly but shown no emotion. The next one had emotion to spare: Daisy had to keep swatting his hands away. Her current dance partner kept stepping on her toes. More than once Daisy had glanced toward Emma and rolled her eyes in frustration.

Emma smiled encouragement. Daisy might not find a love connection at the ball, but she at least was doing something she enjoyed. One thing was certain: the sisters had gone to a lot of effort to create a different spin on the classic Valentine's Day celebration. Supposedly, the doors opened to rooms that were decorated to resemble classic romantic fantasies, such as a castle in Scotland or a gondola ride in nineteenth-century Venice.

But as far as Emma was concerned, the evening was a colossal disaster. She wasn't remotely attracted to any of the men who'd asked her to dance. She'd declined numerous offers, using the excuse that her shoes pinched her feet. The thought of a fantasy adventure with a stranger made her physically ill. If only Björn had come…

The band started to play "Love Takes Time" by Mariah Carey. Emma stifled a sarcastic laugh. The words were an understatement. She felt as though she'd been waiting her whole life. Why did falling in love come easily to others, while in her case it was complicated?

As though to flaunt her point, a couple whirled past her on the dance floor in a blur of red and green. The man was dressed in a Scottish tartan and the woman wore a gown in the style of a noble woman of the Middle Ages. They looked at each other as though they were the only ones in the room. More couples in love twirled past Emma in a sea of color.

Emma stepped back until she'd cleared the dance floor and stood on the perimeter, away from the couples. Her momentary calm evaporated as the music increased in tempo and volume until the sound was deafening as the couples drew closer and closer to her. The noise grated against her skin as she pressed against the wall. She had to get out of here.

A doorknob pressed against her back. Written over the door in script were the words *Chocolate Fantasy*. Daisy had mentioned the matchmaker's flyer advertised that the doors in the café opened into rooms that recreated a time or place. Escaping into a make-believe world seemed the perfect solution.

Emma seized the opportunity to leave, reached behind her, and turned the handle. It was unlocked. A sense of relief, like a breath of clean air, washed over her. Escape.

On the dance floor, Daisy and her newest partner glided past Emma. Daisy had exchanged partners again and was dancing with a man Emma thought looked remarkably like her imaginary boyfriend in the silver photo: Jared Montgomery. Daisy and the Jared look-alike gazed into each other's eyes as though they were the only ones in the room. Emma shook away the illusion. It must be the dim light. It didn't matter what the guy looked like. All that mattered was that Daisy looked giddy with happiness. The couple twirled around the chocolate fountain and out of sight.

But Emma knew her friend. Daisy wouldn't ignore the obvious fact that Emma was still alone. When Daisy and her mystery man reemerged, she would be over here, asking Emma questions. Why wasn't she dancing? Had she heard from Björn? Questions were the last thing Emma needed right now.

If she left while Daisy and the mystery man were on the other side of the room, Emma might have a chance. Sure, Daisy would be upset, but she'd get over it eventually. Daisy never stayed mad longer than it took to bake a batch of cookies. In fact, that had been their friendship pact when they'd first met. Whenever they had a disagreement, they'd bake. Sometimes it took until the last batch was out of the oven, cooled and frosted, but never longer. If Emma did leave the party, it might take baking a double batch before Daisy spoke to her. But one thing Emma knew for sure: she had to leave.

She turned the knob again and opened the door.

Chapter Eighteen

On the threshold, mist blinded her for a moment, taking her by surprise. Disoriented, she took another step. The smell of chocolate greeted Emma like a close friend. People, dressed as though they were auditioning for an eighteenth-century movie, gathered around tables, sipping cups of dark chocolate. The reenactment was flawless: not an electrical device in sight. The sisters had done their homework. This looked like a recreation of one of the French chocolate houses she'd read about on her visit to Paris. In fact, this one was vaguely familiar.

Emma threaded around the tables until she reached the end of a long glass display case.

"*Puis-je vous aider, mademoiselle?*" the man behind the counter said in a thick French accent.

She was surprised that after all this time she understood him completely. He asked her if he could help her. "*Oui. Une table, s'il vous plaît,*" she responded, knowing her accent was rusty, even though after her trip to Paris she had been obsessed with learning how to speak French like a native. The man showed her to a small corner table with the promise that someone would return and take her order.

Snatches of conversation caught her attention. The corrupt and decadent court of Louis XVI and Marie Antoinette was on everyone's mind. A few spoke in hushed tones about the need for revolution, while one couple bent their heads together terrified that his rich wife would discover their affair. Emma was impressed. The scripted conversations further enhanced the illusion of eighteenth-century France.

One thing was certain. She could taste the unrest in the air. She hoped leaving the ball would have distracted her from her loneliness. Instead, she'd stumbled into a place with more couples and been seated at a table for one. She didn't know what she was looking for, but she knew she wouldn't find it here. It would be better if she just went home before a waiter appeared to take her order.

She left her table and headed to a side door.

But instead of entering the Matchmaker Café, she was under a bridge. What was going on? She climbed stone stairs beside the bridge until she reached the street and found herself in an area where buildings rose on either side. Nothing looked familiar. Clouds smothered the stars and moon, plunging the night into a rolling sea of ebony black mist.

Emma rubbed her arms against the sudden chill and turned in a circle. It was so dark she didn't have a sense of where she was in the Village. She felt confused. Which direction was the café? Or her bakery, for that matter? She blew on her hands, debating whether she should go back inside. When she'd first arrived at the Matchmaker Café this afternoon, the weather had seemed more benign, soft and gentle, even. Now it was angry.

She rubbed her arms again. She hadn't thought this through. She'd left without a coat, purse, or cell phone. It was a miracle she had remembered her shoes.

Brilliant.

Emma turned around and retraced her steps, feeling her way over the coarse exterior of the building beside her. Odd. She'd thought all of the retail stores in the Village were made of wood...and where was the door? Hadn't she walked only a few feet away, at most?

Frustrated, she continued to inch along the stone wall. When the rough exterior turned smooth, she took a moment to calm her racing pulse. It was a door, except she couldn't locate the knob. She shouted for help and pounded against the wood, but her voice sounded muffled, swallowed the instant she spoke. She shouted for help again. No one answered.

"Get a grip," she said aloud through chattering teeth. "You're not lost. You're in the Village." She took a deep breath. Perfect. Now she was talking to herself.

She wrapped her arms around her waist, planning her next move. As soon as she left the alley there would be streetlights, cars, and signs directing her to the Matchmaker Café. All she needed to do was sneak back inside, get her coat and purse, and slip out without being noticed. The worst that could happen was she'd catch a cold. After she collected her things and returned home, she and Gigi would fix a batch of chocolate no-bake cookies. She'd explain to Daisy in the morning that she'd tried, but parties weren't for her. In the morning, she'd deal with how she felt about Björn, as well.

"Miss Grey," a man with a Scottish accent said. "Do you need assistance?"

Caught off guard by the stranger, she pressed against the building. The man sounded nice. He didn't sound like a serial killer. The suspicious side of her made a snarky comment: How would she know what a serial killer sounded like?

He lifted a lantern, and the light spilled out like a beacon. "It's William. I work for the sisters and handed you a flyer for the Valentine's Day Ball."

It was the Sean Connery lookalike. Emma nodded, letting out her breath. "It's great to see you. Can you help me? I'm all turned around."

William held the lantern a little higher as he guided her out of the alley toward a horse-drawn carriage. "You look frozen," he said. "But I promise my carriage is so warm you'll think you are sitting in front of a roaring fire."

"Wait. Why do we need a carriage? The café shouldn't be too far away." Emma turned in a slow circle. The darkness had swallowed the white lights throughout the village, making visibility difficult. Cold air crept into her bones, and she scrunched her eyebrows together. "Where's the café?"

"We're too far away, lassie." William held the door open and helped her up the steps and into the carriage. He tucked a blanket around her legs. "Don't worry. I'll take you where you need to go."

William hadn't exaggerated. It was so warm and cozy inside she half expected to see a miniature fireplace with gently rolling flames. Covered in a cocoon of warm blankets, she had no sooner settled back against the cushions than the carriage lurched forward.

Chapter Nineteen

Romance swept through the Matchmaker Café. The music blended with laughter and conversation, creating a unique melody. New couples explored possibilities while established relationships deepened. Things were going according to plan. A perfect party, executed flawlessly. Any party planner would consider this Valentine's Day Ball already a success, believing that nothing could go wrong.

But ensuring that true love blossomed into a forever-after relationship was the tricky part, which was why Lady Roselyn was on edge. She couldn't relax until at least one couple either professed their love or announced their engagement. Then the sisters' obligation as matchmakers would be fulfilled and their license renewed for another year. She opened a large box of assorted chocolate truffles and added them to a nearly empty dessert tray.

It took all three sisters to ensure success. Fiona's gift was identifying when two people were poised to open their hearts. Lady Roselyn and Bridget's gifts were more practical in nature, but of late Bridget had showed glimpses that she might be more like their mother. Another worry.

Lady Roselyn opened another box to refill the next tray as Bridget approached. Lady Roselyn paused and braced herself. Everything about Bridget looked tense.

"Have we run out of food?"

"Why did you send Emma through the door that would place her on the eve of the French Revolution?"

"You're mistaken. Emma went through the door that leads to the grand opening of the Moulin Rouge in Paris in eighteen eighty-nine. Such a fun time. Can-can, lively music…"

"Police raids."

"I'm ignoring you," Lady Roselyn said. "I sent Fiona there to guide Emma. Bridget will instruct Björn when he arrives."

"I talked to Fiona. Emma never arrived at the Moulin Rouge. She went through the wrong door."

Lady Roselyn's hands trembled, and the box of truffles slipped from her grasp. Of all the things she worried about, having someone waltz through one of their doors unsupervised ranked in the top five. But that was impossible. Bridget must be mistaken. There were so many safeguards.

Convinced her sister was wrong, she dropped down to clean up the truffles. "Oh, bother. Look what you made me do. You're mistaken. What you're saying is impossible. The doors leading to France should all have been locked, except for the one I intended for Emma to find. You're mistaken," she repeated.

Bridget knelt beside Lady Roselyn and covered her sister's hand with her own. "There's no mistake. Daisy noticed Emma leave through our French Revolution door and came to tell me. She thought Emma had agreed on a fantasy after all."

"This is a disaster." Lady Roselyn looked up, scanning the doors that lined the walls of the café. Hours ago, she had been proud of their collection. The age of the doors ranged from the present to one they believed once had stood in a home in Pompeii before Mt. Vesuvius had destroyed the city. Panic clutched at her throat. How had this happened?

"Are they all locked now?" Lady Roselyn said shoving smashed truffles into her box as her apprehension grew.

Bridget nodded, helping her sister pick up the mess. "I double-checked myself."

Lady Roselyn stood slowly, reciting a litany of Irish proverbs in her head to calm her fears. They'd never allowed a couple to travel back in time unsupervised. She'd learned that lesson the hard way. "Well, it's done," Lady Roselyn said. "Someone must go after her."

Bridget wiped the chocolate off her hands with a napkin. "Liam sent William in right away to buy us some time and then came to find me. Then he and Andrew followed. Björn had just arrived, asking for Emma, so everything fell into place quickly. We used a version of the damsel-in-distress scenario, and while Björn changed into appropriate clothes for the century, I filled him in on what to expect."

Lady Roselyn stood up straighter. "Wait. Did you say Andrew is here? Why didn't you tell me?"

"Like I said. Everything was happening so fast, and Andrew said he had it under control."

Lady Roselyn clenched her teeth together and rubbed her temples. She would deal with Andrew later. "You explained to Björn that although where he was going looked real, it was just a reenactment?"

Bridget hesitated. "Of course."

"Of course," Lady Roselyn repeated. Her heart

raced like she'd finished a marathon, or like the time she'd fought in the Irish rebellion. What else could possibly go wrong?

Chapter Twenty

The carriage came to an abrupt stop, waking Emma from a sound sleep. She settled back against the seat cushions and yawned. She must have dozed off. She had been having such a lovely dream. In her dream, Björn had arrived late to the Valentine's Day Ball and had asked her to dance. The dream had brought back memories of her senior prom.

They both had been so nervous. Björn had asked her to dance then, too, but when a slow dance started, he disappeared. By the time he returned, she'd made up her mind. He had made the noble gesture by asking her to the prom when he learned her date had stood her up, but the intimacy of a slow dance must have freaked him out. She hadn't wanted to lose their friendship, so she'd accepted a dance with a guy from her math class.

Wondering why the carriage was stopped, she yawned again and swept aside the curtains over the window. Had they arrived at the café or her boulangerie finally?

The storm clouds had cleared a path through the night sky and exposed an expanse of moon and stars. On either side of the street, gas street lamps illuminated three-story and four-story buildings that looked like something from a French postcard. Arched doorways framed with elaborate swirls and columns only added to Emma's confusion. She had wanted to go home. Had

William misunderstood and driven her to a reenactment site? The sisters had claimed that their reenactments looked real. That had been an understatement.

She leaned out the window to get a better look. Blocking the carriage was a masked man astride a black horse. His cape flowed behind him in the wind as he aimed a rifle toward William. She pulled back into the shadows of the carriage.

If she hadn't known better, she'd have sworn she was still dreaming. The man held an antique weapon that looked like all the cliché images of highwaymen she had seen in movies or read about in novels. The sisters' reenactments were designed to make their clients believe they'd stepped into another time and place, and it sure appeared as though they'd pulled it off.

Curious, she peered out the window again.

"I heard you were transporting a French noble." The man's voice rumbled like angry thunder. He nodded to William. "Turn the woman over to me, and I'll spare your life."

Emma stifled her giggles, feeling her anxiety calm. Obviously, the sisters were behind this reenactment. Even though the dialogue and the French accent sounded a little over the top, being abducted by what she suspected was a French revolutionist was an intriguing plot idea. She, of course, would play the part of the fleeing noblewoman. If only the man were…

She shook her head to clear her thoughts. Björn hadn't come to the party, remember? That should tell her all she needed to know about their future together. Maybe she should play along. The guy was attractive, and the sisters had gone to a lot of trouble to make this fantasy feel real. What did she have to lose?

William sat on the driver's bench seat, his hands in the air. The four horses looked calm. One even angled its head around to give her a look, as though to say, *This happens all the time.*

Emma scooted closer to the window to get a better look. The man urged his horse forward until he was peering down at Emma. "Get out," the man bellowed so loud that William flinched. There was a rehearsed quality to the highwayman's behavior, as though he'd played this part before, but his Me-Tarzan-you-Jane attitude didn't work for her anymore, no matter how attractive he was. She didn't have a man in her life, but she wasn't in the mood for a one-night stand, either. And this character had the love-them-and-leave them look written all over his face.

She no longer wanted the broody, misunderstood bad boy who promised to change with the love of the right woman beside him. Emma had dated those high-maintenance types in her twenties. In her thirties, she wanted something better. The sisters had completely misunderstood her fantasy type.

Emma wanted a man who could stand on his own and wanted and respected a woman who did the same. She wanted someone like Björn, not a cave-dwelling Neanderthal. The realization came so clearly it took her breath away. But did Björn feel the same way? What was the real reason he hadn't come to the party?

Regardless, she wasn't going to waste her time with this guy. She'd tell William to take her home, and in the morning, she'd let the sisters know she appreciated their efforts.

The door to the carriage slammed open. The force

rocked the coach as the man reached in and yanked her to the ground. "I told you. Get out." He turned on William. "Leave."

William hesitated as though he wanted to say something but seemed to change his mind. He cracked the reins over the horses' rumps and sped out of sight. The horses' hooves echoed over the cobblestones as the carriage disappeared into the mist.

She scrambled to her feet and brushed leaves off her dress, choking on the dust of the departing carriage. Her hands stung, and it was cold without the protection of the blankets in the carriage. She rubbed her arms. But both discomforts were the least of her concerns. She couldn't believe William had left her with this cave dweller.

Stay calm, she ordered. She'd express to the revolutionist that she wasn't interested in his brand of fantasy. Then she'd ask him if he'd give her a ride home or return her to the café, whichever was faster. She'd never ridden a horse, but if the guy went slow, how hard could it be?

When he reached for her arm, his grip was not gentlemanly. She jerked out of his reach. "Hey. Not a fan of being manhandled." She stepped back. This guy would not get a glowing report. "I'm not interested in whatever this is. Take me home. Now."

He hesitated and glanced in the direction William had headed, then holstered his weapon and withdrew a leather strap from his belt. "Those weren't my instructions." His voice was a low rumble of anger laced with the confidence of a man used to having his own way. He grabbed her by the wrist. "I'm taking you, but not home."

A chill caused an involuntary shudder up her spine. He was taking the reenactment too seriously. She tried to pull away, but his grip bit into her flesh. Her mind raced. She couldn't believe the sisters thought this scenario would be her fantasy. She scanned the area and for the first time realized it was too quiet. Where was the Village? The town? Traffic? William must have driven her to a remote location in the country. About thirty or more miles from Seattle, a nonprofit organization had built a medieval village. Perhaps the organization had also built one for the French Revolution and the sisters were using it for the ball.

"Hold still," he ordered.

"You don't have to take me back. I can find my way on my own."

"I said, hold still."

"So you can tie me up? No, thanks." Emma tried to twist out of his grasp. His grip was viselike and his expression deadly calm. Ice-cold fear raced through her as warning bells went off in her head. The reenactment had taken a dark turn.

His brows knitted together as he yanked her toward him. "I thought you'd be a screamer. Why aren't you screaming?" He looked disappointed and something else.

He swore under his breath and with his free hand drew his pistol, aimed it at the sky, and pulled the trigger. The weapon discharged smoke and a pop so loud her ears rang. His horse reared up and bolted in the direction William had fled and was swallowed up by the same mist.

The man swore another string of oaths, some in a language she didn't understand, and leveled his gaze.

"And still she doesn't scream. I'm getting too old for this." Still holding onto her, he pointed his weapon at the sky and pulled the trigger again. It sounded even louder the second time.

Emma flinched and froze in place. This guy was a certifiable nut case.

"That better do it," he said, holstering his pistol again. He heaved a sigh and shouted, "It will go easier if you don't resist."

She would not be intimidated. "Anyone who believes that line is an idiot."

He looked like he was about to respond and thought she noticed his lip curl as though he were about to smile. Pausing, he lifted his gaze. "Did you hear something?" His expression relaxed. "Finally." He released her, reaching for a section of rope looped over his belt. "Turn around. I'm going to tie you up."

Every horror, mystery, or scary movie Emma had ever watched flashed through her thoughts. The villains always said those exact words, and until recently, the heroines rarely fought back.

Emma channeled her inner Wonder Woman, grabbed handfuls of her dress, hiked it up, and kneed him between the legs.

Startled, his expression told her she'd hit the mark. As he groaned in pain and bent over, she shoved him away and turned.

And ran straight into Björn.

Björn swept her behind him, his face a mask of concern. "Are you okay?"

"What are you doing here?"

The man struggled to stand straight, breathing as though he'd run a marathon. "The woman comes with me," he said between breaths.

"I don't think so," Björn said evenly. He balled his fist and hit the man in the jaw. The man's eyes widened for a moment as his hand hovered over his gun. A muscle twitched along Björn's jaw as he hit the man again.

Chapter Twenty-One

Björn draped his jacket over Emma's shoulders, keeping an eye on the highwayman. It had been a long time since he'd been in a bar fight. At the time, he'd blamed his wild side, or the combination of being young, alive, and living in the adrenaline rush that was Alaska, or because it was a Tuesday. Back then it didn't take much to excuse his behavior.

He'd left that life behind when he stopped drinking. But even if that life was in the past, there were a few things you didn't forget, and one was being able to size up your opponent. Björn looked over his shoulder at the unconscious highwayman. The guy had gone down too easily.

Emma tugged on his sleeve. "We should leave before he wakes up. Do you know where we are?"

Unfortunately, he did. Explaining it was another issue. "First we need to get off the street. I had a difficult time believing where I was when I first arrived."

That was an understatement. When Bridget had told him that Emma was in trouble, he hadn't hesitated and had been only half-listening to her tall tale. Something about time travel and doors that opened into the past. It wasn't until he'd stepped through the door to this place—and been engulfed in turbulence that made a storm off the coast of Alaska feel like a ripple in a bathtub—that it had hit him.

Bridget was telling the truth.

He hadn't had time to panic. He was too busy locating Emma.

Björn put his hand on the back of Emma's waist and guided her in the direction of a narrow street. He'd seen a lot of strange things, fishing in Alaska. When he'd fallen overboard, a shark had swum in for the attack only to be chased away by a dolphin and some killer whales, or Orcas as they are known in the Pacific Northwest. They were swimming alongside the boat as unofficial protectors. But that paled compared to what he and Emma now faced. How did you tell someone they'd traveled back in time and landed almost in the French Revolution?

Beneath a street lamp, vendors were gathering up their merchandise. Wicker baskets, miniature windmills, stoneware, and lanterns were either packed in wheelbarrows or small carts. Emma glanced in the direction of the vendors with the same wide-eyed expression he knew he must have had the first time he'd seen them. The merchants should be selling knockoff Prada and Gucci purses or Rolex watches, not lanterns.

Emma turned toward him, her eyes wide. "This looks too…"

"Real," he finished, knowing exactly how freaked out she felt. "We have a way to go yet. I passed a restaurant where I can try and explain what's happened."

Emma crossed her arms over her chest, for all the world like someone who would not go another step. "Explain. Now."

Björn glanced toward the vendors. A few of them

had looked up from dismantling their stalls to stare over at Emma and Björn. "We should discuss this someplace else. There's the restaurant I mentioned, where we can talk."

"I have a better idea. Let's return to the Matchmaker Café."

"That's what I've been trying to explain. We can't return. At least not yet, anyway. And when we do, we must find a door that has a Scottish thistle. Bridget said it has something to do with the rules of the enchantment. We can enter most of the doors at any time, but we can only return to our own time at the stroke of midnight."

Emma narrowed her gaze. "Like Cinderella and her pumpkin coach?"

"Sounds about right."

"Are you delusional? That makes no sense."

Björn pulled her a short distance away from the curious vendors. "Please, lower your voice. This is not a good place for us to draw attention to ourselves."

She yanked out of his grasp. "Fine. But stop saying crazy stuff. I'm tired and…"

"You're tired because we time traveled. Bridget said that might happen."

"You're starting to worry me. I'll find my own way back."

He blocked her path. "I didn't want to believe it when Bridget first told me. Look around you. The sisters bragged that they created reenactments, but it's all too perfect. The people. This place. Think about it. How could something this elaborate and large go unnoticed? We are in seventeen hundred eighty-nine, on the eve of the French Revolution, and I understand every word of French being spoken."

Her eyes hardened. "That's impossible. The only foreign language you took in school was German."

Björn looked over his shoulder. The vendors had started to inch their way toward them. "Bridget said that's part of the enchantment. Once we cross over the threshold, we can understand the language of the time in history we entered. Wait. Are those men carrying pitchforks and torches?"

Emma rolled her eyes. "Seriously?" But she stepped around him and did a double-take as though seeing the vendors for the first time. Her breath came faster and faster, and then she did something very un-Emma-like. She fainted into Björn's arms.

Chapter Twenty-Two

Emma still felt shaky and numb and embarrassed. She'd never fainted. To make matters worse, Björn stood beside her, watching over her as though she were made of glass. Somewhere between the narrow street where she'd fainted and the place where she now stood, Björn had set her down in front of what looked like some sort of restaurant. The façade of the building was painted green and gold, but the name of the establishment was obscured by shadows.

The dark sky was overcast, and the gas streetlamps provided the only light filtering through the dense fog that rolled in from the River Seine. Occasionally, a horse-drawn carriage would clip-clop past them, or policemen would whistle and chase after someone who'd broken the law. From her time in Paris she remembered that the police were called *gendarmerie.*

Björn had said they'd time-traveled. The whole concept sounded insane. She replayed conversations she'd had with the sisters, as he'd suggested. The sisters advertised that their matchmaker business was all about granting fantasy romances for their couples. She hadn't thought anything of their claim. The world was already littered with businesses offering the same types of things. One of her favorite movies was *Austenland* with Keri Russell, where the premise was that guests could purchase a vacation where they'd visit an estate in

England and dress in Regency costumes, pretending to be characters from the Jane Austen novels. There was even a Mr. Darcy. But…time travel?

Armed soldiers, wearing long navy jackets over white, close-fitting pants, red plumes on their hats, jogged past her on the cobblestones. Their uniforms and the surrounding area looked too perfect to be part of an elaborate reenactment.

A horse-drawn coach with a suspended carriage and plush red velvet interior pulled up alongside the restaurant. The driver jumped down and opened the door for the couple inside. The man stepped out, wearing a cream-colored waistcoat over thigh-hugging breeches with blue-and-white-striped silk hose. He reached into the carriage to help the woman. She ducked her head to allow her headdress to clear the opening. A bird's nest rested in the towering structure piled on top of her head, complete with blue robin's eggs, multi-colored butterflies, and a stuffed squirrel. The forest theme was reflected in the fabric of her gown and matching high-heeled shoes. The woman paused to take in Emma's simpler choice before entering the restaurant.

"This is really happening." Emma shivered as the door closed and wafted a whiff of familiar scent her way. "You came after me."

"Bridget knew my Achilles' heel," he said, "and her name is Emma Gray. When I couldn't find you at the ball, I asked around, and that's when I ran into Bridget and she told me where you'd gone. Things happened pretty fast after that, and here I am."

She loved that he had come after her and that she had her own personal knight in shining armor. No matter how independent a woman became, there was that appreciation for a guy who wanted to be by her side when things were difficult. Björn had always been that type of man even if she'd had to be yanked out of her world into another to help her realize it.

But time travel?

The bigger question was how was it even possible? One minute she was standing in the Matchmaker Café, and the next, she'd walked over a threshold into another century. She hadn't been transported back in time in an H. G. Wells time machine or used a Star Trek-style space ship to warp speed into the past. She'd just walked.

Emma had asked about a door in the café the sisters said they'd acquired from an estate in France where Julia Child and her husband had once lived. If Emma had opened that door, would she have met Julia herself?

"You're pretty quiet," Björn said, interrupting her thoughts.

She cleared her throat. "Do you think we lost the highwayman who attacked us?" It was not the question she wanted to ask, but it felt the safest. She wanted to ask how they were going to make it back to their own century.

"Hope so." Björn stood close by. It's how she remembered him in school. He was there if she, or anyone else for that matter, needed him.

Björn had always been tall for his age, and he had used that to his advantage whenever someone had been bullied in school. He'd learned early that most bullies were cowards, so all he had to do was stand beside the harassed victim, and the bully would back down.

She was grateful for his company. But this wasn't high school. And if Björn was right—and she was beginning to believe he was—this was Paris, not as it was in the twenty-first century, but in the eighteenth.

Police whistles pierced the chill air, and there were shouts of someone being chased. She shivered, pulling Björn's coat tighter around her shoulders. The night seemed to close in around her. What must Björn be thinking of her? She'd fainted. Seriously? And he was so patient. Another one of his good qualities. But there were times when she'd wanted him not to be so patient. What was he waiting for? Was it really patience, or was it fear of commitment that held him back? And why hadn't he ever tried to kiss her?

Björn continued to stand nearby, patiently watching as though she might faint again or start screaming. She had to admit the screaming part was tempting, and not because they'd time-traveled.

"Are you okay?" Björn said.

"Peachy. What do we do next?"

"We're supposed to find out where Marie Antoinette's party is being held. According to Bridget, there is a door at that location that opens at midnight and leads back to the Matchmaker Café."

She stepped aside as the restaurant door opened and two men dressed in black coats exited. She caught the familiar scent again. Was that chocolate? One of the men tipped his hat before following his comrade down the sidewalk, and then they turned to stare at Emma and Björn before disappearing around the corner.

Standing out in the street was drawing too much attention. They were strangers in a world they barely understood. "We should head to this place Bridget mentioned. Do we have an address?" she said, lowering her voice.

"More like bread crumbs." He reached into his jacket and pulled out a slip of paper with written instructions. "The first on the list is the street where your coach was attacked. The next one is this restaurant, 30 Rue des Saints-Peres, on the Left Bank. We have instructions to order something to eat and then wait for the next clue."

The door opened again, and a laughing couple, dressed in clothing befitting people who belonged to the French elite, walked out arm in arm.

"Did I smell chocolate?" Emma said, taking in the rich aromas coming from inside the restaurant.

Björn chuckled under his breath. "And she's back. I noticed this place when I first arrived. With a lot of people, retail therapy calms the nerves. For my Emma, it's chocolate."

Chapter Twenty-Three

As Emma entered the restaurant, Björn's words folded around her like a soft caress. He'd said, "My Emma." Did the words mean what she hoped they meant? She shook herself free of them and the wishful implications.

The inside of the crowded shop was like a miniature palace with high ceilings, crystal chandeliers, marble pillars, and gold-trimmed molding and furnishings. Silk upholstered chairs clustered around small tables where couples drank tea or sipped drinking chocolate while they indulged in decadent-looking desserts.

The smell of chocolate was the only thing that was familiar. She gave a quick glance over her shoulder at the entrance before turning back. Björn had said it was on the Left Bank along the Seine River. Why hadn't she made the connection sooner?

"I've been here before," Emma said more to herself than to Björn. "This is the Debauve and Gallais chocolate house. Salpice Debauve invented chocolate coins for Marie Antoinette. She didn't like her medicine, and the coins helped disguise the taste. She was so impressed, she declared Debauve the royal chocolatier."

Björn grinned. "Is there anything about chocolate you don't know?" Not waiting for her answer, he said,

"You say this place is still here in our time?"

She nodded, feeling as though she were being pulled into the shop's embrace.

"There's something I have to do," he said. "I'll be right back."

She nodded again, only half hearing what he'd said as she moved to stand in line behind several couples waiting either to be seated or to place their order at the counter. The magical smells of cocoa in all its forms filled the warm, compact space. Björn was right: for some reason the recognizable scents calmed her. She picked up the aromas of vanilla, cinnamon, and orange, and then detected walnuts, almonds, and the faint smell of chilies.

Well, if they had to wait somewhere, this certainly seemed like the ideal spot. The opportunity to taste-test desserts made during the eighteenth century chased away all her previous anxieties. There were people who participated in the wine tastings at Washington State's over eight hundred wineries. Emma had never had the time or interest, but the chance to indulge in chocolate tastings was something else entirely.

With a lightness in her step, she moved closer to the counter as the line inched forward.

A few minutes later, Björn rejoined her and placed his hand at her arm, gently holding her back. "I'm not sure this was a good idea after all. I didn't see the highwayman, but he may have followed us here and be waiting somewhere outside."

She glanced over her shoulder at him. He looked so cute, playing the role of protector. It brought back every fantasy she'd ever had of him when she was growing up. She knew it was irrational, but she wasn't afraid if he was beside her. She didn't want to believe that this heightened awareness was all part of the danger they were experiencing together, but she couldn't rule it out. When they returned to their lives, would things go back to the way they were? She'd plunge herself into her bakery and he'd return to Alaska? Or would this experience move them beyond friendship?

But maybe even that didn't matter. Maybe for some people the memories of a few magical moments were enough. She was over-thinking, that was certain. Time to live in the moment.

Embracing this theory, she said, "A highwayman in a chocolate shop? I doubt that seriously. Those types hang out in taverns or pubs. Besides, we must stay here. You said it yourself that we have to wait here for the next clue." She stood on tiptoes and kissed him on the cheek.

He seemed startled. "Why did you kiss me?"

She shrugged, inching forward in line again. She loved that she'd taken him by surprise. She loved even more that he didn't appear annoyed. In fact, was there heightened color in his face? "I couldn't help myself," she admitted. "I blame the chocolate. It makes me want to do things completely out of character. Does that ever happen to you?" When he didn't answer, she took it as a no and continued, "Did you know that when chocolate was first brought to Europe, the Catholic Church considered it an aphrodisiac and therefore too dangerous for women to consume? Even the aroma puts us fragile creatures in a romantic mood."

He winked. "I take it that made chocolate more popular than ever."

"You made a joke? There is hope for you yet, Mr.

Erikson."

"You bring out the best in me. How many chocolate shops are there in Paris?"

Emma turned toward him, feeling as though her face were lit with smiles. "Dozens, maybe hundreds. Chocolate has been popular in France since the sixteen hundreds, when King Louis XIII married a Spanish princess who gave him chocolate as a wedding present."

"I've never understood the obsession. To me, one candy bar tastes the same as another."

"I can't believe you just said that." Emma giggled and put her finger to her mouth and made a shushing sound. "You shouldn't say things like that too loudly. Someone might hear you. What you said might be considered a hanging offense in France. In Paris, they'd probably use the guillotine and lop off your head."

"You're joking?"

"Only a little," she said with a laugh. "Come with me. It's time to give you a new outlook on life. You've spent your life trying to explain to me that not all fish tastes the same. To try and prove your point, you, your dad, and your brothers barbequed a feast for my family. There was everything from King, Copper River, and Coho salmon to swordfish, halibut, Petrale sole, and red snapper. I've never felt so full in my life."

He shrugged. "We may have gone a little overboard. You never did tell me your favorite."

"Your mom changed my mind about Brussels sprouts. Does that count? She tossed them with cooked bacon bits, brown sugar, and spices, and roasted them on the barbeque. They were so good I asked your mother for the recipe."

"That's was your favorite? The vegetables? That's not funny."

"It's a little funny." She grinned, teasing him. She loved how his eyes crinkled at the corners and how his brows knit together when he was trying to be serious. He usually fooled everyone. Not her. The expression in his eyes was a dead giveaway.

She sucked in a deep breath. "We're next," she said, trying to focus on something other than the way Björn was looking at her. She didn't want to read something that might not be there. "Prepare to have your world rocked. Chocolate is every bit as complex as winemaking," she said, trying to ignore how warm his gaze made her feel. She instructed herself to breathe as she moved toward the counter.

"Cocoa beans around the world," she continued, "are combined for the best flavor by expert chocolatiers. They combine the strong bean varieties from Cuba, Trinidad, and Grenada with the milder varieties from Jamaica and Sri Lanka for a signature blend. Chocolatiers, like winemakers, study for years to perfect their craft."

He bent forward and kissed her.

A wave of heat surged through her, and her face warmed under his touch. The kiss lingered long enough to send delicious shudders through her body. She repeated the same words he'd said to her moments before. "Why did you kiss me?"

Chapter Twenty-Four

They were still in line, but Björn didn't mind. He also hadn't answered Emma's question. The truth was that he wasn't sure why he'd kissed her. All he remembered was that while she was talking he had been concentrating on her lips, not her words. He thought he remembered her mentioning something about cocoa beans and chocolatiers.

Then he'd kissed her. An innocent kiss. Except it wasn't innocent. He knew from the jolt that seared through him when their lips met, as well as from her expression and the way she kept talking faster and faster.

Something had shifted between them.

They were finally next in line. Emma approached the counter to place her order with a tall man dressed like a Valentine's Day card. His gloves and waistcoat were candy-apple red, his breeches were purple striped, and his silk hose pink.

Everywhere Björn looked, couples were seated at tables or stood sipping chocolate or eating desserts. Emma had told him they'd be taste-testing chocolate. The irony was that the way he was feeling, she could have asked him if he wanted to sample baked grasshoppers, roasted ants, or fried spiders rolled in crushed cockroaches and he would have agreed. Emma was animated and excited. He hadn't seen her this way in a long time.

Emma had reminded him of all the fish she'd eaten the day his father had barbequed. Björn had another memory. That day had been a group effort and one of his fondest memories. Emma and both their mothers had prepared the side dishes. His mother had announced that the men would oversee cleaning and preparing the fish. Björn agreed the menfolk had gotten a little carried away with the amount they had planned to cook and ended up with enough fish to feed a boatload of hungry fishermen. His parents had solved the problem by inviting their friends from the Village to join in the feast. Laughing with Emma and enjoying the camaraderie of family and friends that afternoon were some of his best memories. The food was a distant second.

Björn watched as Emma chatted with the man behind the counter. He had introduced himself as Claude. Claude and Emma carried on an animated conversation as she selected a variety of chocolates. A few times Claude shook his head, but Emma pressed. Björn had learned early that when Emma became passionate about a subject she didn't give up until she won the argument. Björn smiled to himself. Claude didn't have a chance.

He remembered an argument he and Emma had had over a young woman he'd dated in high school. Emma had claimed Tiffany was cheating on him with his best friend. The accusation had hit him like a blow to the gut, but he had known Emma was right even before he confronted them.

When he and Tiffany broke up, he considered asking Emma out on a real date. He'd finally realized that his feelings for her went way beyond friendship. But he'd reconsidered. He hadn't wanted to risk their friendship.

"Are you ready?" Emma asked.

He straightened. "Excuse me?"

"Are you ready for a taste test?" Emma gave a quick nod to a silver platter on the counter. It held a display of chocolate in different shapes, sizes, and shades from dark to light. She was beaming like the proverbial kid in a candy shop. A short distance away, Claude was preparing a table in a remote corner of the café. He'd removed the center candle and replaced it with a round, ceramic bowl that rested on an iron platform over a warming candle. The setting was intimate and romantic.

Over the years, Björn had visualized what it would be like if he ever did have the courage to ask Emma out on a first date. His grand plan ranged from dinner and a movie. Imagination was never his strong suit. Nowhere in his wildest dreams would he have come up with the combination of chocolate and Paris.

"Too much?" Emma said, gazing up at him, her eyes wide with unspoken questions. She tore from his gaze to stare in the direction of Claude. "I may have lost control."

Every fiber of his being wanted to disagree and shout that it might be a good idea for them to lose control now and then. Impulsively kissing each other was a great start. People believed because Emma ran her own shop and Björn fished in Alaska that they were risk takers. That couldn't be further from the truth. When it came to matters of the heart, they played it safe.

Björn reached for the silver platter and decided for once to take a leap. "We traveled back in time. Out of control might be our new norm."

Chapter Twenty-Five

Björn followed Emma to the table Claude had set for them. "We have a lot of chocolate."

"This is only the beginning," Emma said with a smile.

Claude pulled out the chair for Emma as Björn sat down opposite her, struggling to adjust his long legs under the table. "We might need a bigger table."

Emma reached for his hand. "Absolutely not. This is cozy." She withdrew her hand and looked over the selection of chocolate. "This is so much fun. Claude said the French consider chocolate a medicine that can cure everything from chronic illness to a broken heart. There is also a story about women in a small town who claimed they couldn't sit through the long mass service without the help of their cup of hot cocoa. The priests eventually gave in, but it was quite the scandal." She selected one of the chocolates and held it toward Björn. "You should try this one first. Claude said it's called a truffle because it is made to look like the round black mushrooms from Périgord. These are dark chocolate and rolled in cocoa powder."

Before he could ask why someone would name candy after mushrooms that were dug up out of the ground, she popped the truffle into his mouth. He swallowed it down whole as though it were a pill. "Good."

Emma frowned and cocked her head. "Good? What does that mean? You ate it so fast I doubt you had time to taste the rose cream inside. What did you feel? Can you detect any characteristics? Cinnamon? Black cherry? Almonds?" When he didn't answer, she gave Björn an exasperated look and chose another one from the platter. "Try this one," she said as she placed it in his mouth. "Please. Eat this one slowly."

He had absolutely no clue what he was supposed to feel about eating candy so sugary sweet he could almost hear his dentist's lecture. Björn did, however, know exactly how he felt about Emma feeding him chocolate. He held her gaze as he forced himself to eat slowly. A delicate pink glow brushed over her skin. He smiled and her blush deepened.

"Well?" she said, her voice as rich as the chocolate he'd eaten.

This time he made sure he didn't respond too fast. "Okay, this time I could taste the cinnamon."

She tilted her head and her hand poised over the tray of chocolates as though considering her choices. She zeroed in on a dark truffle rolled in powdered sugar. "Nice try, big guy. The one I gave you was seventy percent dark chocolate with a hint of orange zest. There wasn't so much as a pinch of cinnamon. But I appreciate the effort. You are still eating too fast. Your mother used to say that you and your brothers never tasted food, you just inhaled and swallowed." She took a bite of the truffle she'd selected, closed her eyes, and moaned.

His brain stopped working.

Emma was a different person away from her bakery. He didn't know why they'd ended up being stuck back in time, but he was beginning to be very, very grateful.

Claude brought a pitcher of liquid chocolate over to the table, another waiter brought a platter of cake cut into bite-sized pieces, while another waiter lit the warming candle under the ceramic container. The flurry of activity reminded Björn of a well-run fishing vessel. Everyone knew their assigned tasks.

Claude poured the pitcher of warm chocolate into the container in the center of the table, gave a slight bow, and nodded to his fellow waiters that it was time to leave. Emma reached for a utensil, speared one of the pieces of pound cake, dipped it into the thick chocolate, and then popped the dessert into her mouth. Chocolate dripped from her lips. She flicked some of it from her lips with the tip of her tongue. "Yummy. Try some."

What he wanted to do was kiss the chocolate from her mouth. "I thought fondue was a Swiss thing," he said instead.

She licked her lips free of the chocolate. "It is. I just made a few suggestions."

"Aren't you afraid you're messing with the events in time?"

"Not at all. My mother said the French and Swiss loved exchanging recipes. No one knows for sure who invented the idea of dipping cake and fruit into warmed chocolate. Like so many things, it probably happened by accident. I wish they'd had pineapples or strawberries. I like the fruit better. Maybe when we get back…" Her expression clouded over.

He reached over to squeeze her hand. "We'll make it back."

She hesitated. "Would it be so bad if we didn't?"

She shook her head. "Never mind. Shouldn't we have received the next clue by now?"

Björn kept his hand closed around hers. He knew what she meant. Right now he didn't care if they ever returned. "It's only around seven o'clock or so. We have until midnight."

"That's not an answer."

"You're right. How about this for a plan? We wait here a little longer, and if we still haven't heard anything, we retrace our steps to the location where your coach was attacked. Maybe William has circled back for us and is waiting." He squeezed her hand again. "Now, how about another chocolate lesson?"

Her eyes glistened as she brushed at her cheek. "Remember to eat slowly and think about how it makes you feel."

That was a problem. He already knew how he felt, at least where Emma was concerned. He reached over and brushed a tear from her face. "We're going to be okay. I won't let anything happen to you."

Chapter Twenty-Six

Back at the sisters' Valentine's Day Ball, the music and the couples had slipped into that romantic world of soft melodies and tender whispers. The couples were well matched and having a good time. Fiona wondered if Emma and Björn had made it safely to Marie Antoinette's party. Were Marie's parties as romantic as the history books claimed? One day, she vowed, she would see for herself. The more pressing question revolved round the fact that no one was sure what had caused the mix-up with the doors. If Daisy hadn't seen her friend leave when she did, poor Emma would have been stranded in eighteenth-century France.

Fiona sighed as she carried two glasses of ale over to a small table near the front entrance. For now, she had to stay focused. Already there had been too many unanswered questions. Björn had been given detailed instructions on how to find Emma and then head straight for the chocolate house on the Left Bank and wait for further information on how to proceed. It was too dangerous for them to wander around Paris on their own. Plans were being made for someone to meet them there.

Sometimes the sisters' duties overlapped, but generally, Lady Roselyn oversaw finding and maintaining the physical location of the Matchmaker Café. Fiona usually paired couples, and Bridget created the theme and rules for each party or reenactment. They all decided which doors were needed to accomplish the best results, and William, as hereditary Keeper of the Doors, made sure they were guarded and that no one went through without his knowledge. After tonight's mishap of Emma opening a door that was supposed to be locked, they would have to be more careful.

Fiona glanced toward the window. Although the rain had ceased, the breeze had morphed into a threatening wind that rattled the shutters and scraped the branches against the window panes. It enhanced the drama and kept their guests inside, but weather was difficult to control. It's unpredictability sometimes worked against them.

She smiled softly to herself. And there were times the weather worked its magic. A storm had raged the night she had helped Liam outrun whoever was after them over New Year's. Soaked to the bone, they had escaped to a small cottage on the edge of Inverness, Scotland. Her pulse quickened and her face flushed at the memory of Liam's gentle touch. The intensity of their true feelings for each other had taken them both by surprise. She'd told her sister that she was in love with two men. But was what she felt for Liam real, or was Duncan the man she was supposed to be with?

Duncan was the total fantasy. A real-life knight in shining armor. He even owned a castle. He was also gone most of the time on crusades, or defending his lands. Was that the attraction? A fantasy dream of perfection? She twisted the glass of ale in her hand.

What was keeping Liam? He usually wasn't this late.

In some ways, Liam's role was the most varied

and, therefore, most difficult. It changed with each assignment. Sometimes, Liam played the part of a villain, or more accurately, a highwayman. Other times he was the jilted lover or occasionally went undercover as a street performer who made sure all went well for their guests.

His role in the previous assignment, on New Year's Eve, was of that nature. The adventure had started out routinely, a marriage of convenience that might turn into something more. The match couple, C.C., the woman who owned Sandwich Land in the Village, and Michael Campbell, a professional football quarterback, had faked their marriage in order to repair his image. Liam's assignment had been to keep the match couple safe from the Jacobite uprising.

Then everything had gone wrong. C.C. and Michael had been evading what they presumed were men from the Jacobite rebellion. Liam had prevented the attack but sacrificed his safety, which was how he'd become stranded back in time, and why she'd gone after him.

The German cuckoo clock began its countdown to ten o'clock. She glanced over her shoulder. Liam should have been back by now.

All the matchmaking events held risk. In the case of last year's Christmas adventure, which had followed the story of *Brigadoon* and took place in the thirteenth century, there had been uninvited guests. At New Year's Eve in Inverness, Scotland, they were attacked by the supporters of Bonnie Prince Charlie. That was the reason they'd decided to scale back this year until they discovered who or what was behind the unusual interference at their events.

A knock on the front door drew Fiona's attention. A late arrival perhaps? Liam never knocked, but there was a first time for everything, as the saying went. But when she crossed the room and opened the door, it was William, not a late arrival, who greeted her.

She tried to disguise her disappointment. "How did it go?"

William looked as calm as he always did, as though nothing as ordinary as a storm could ruffle his mood. "Mission accomplished," he said, getting straight to the point. "Liam held up the coach as planned and made a convincing highwayman. I felt terrible leaving Emma behind. The look she gave me…" He shook his head slowly. "But Björn had things well under control."

Fiona put her hand on the man's shoulder. "Don't feel bad. Liam plays his part well. When Emma returns, we'll explain to her that it was all part of the reenactment. Can you stay?"

"Better not. The horses are a bit spooked and need my attention. I'll check in with Lady Roselyn first."

"Good luck finding her," Fiona said, not caring about the bitterness in her voice. "I haven't seen her in over an hour." Sometimes her older sister vanished at the most inopportune times. She knew that the same could be said about her. Maybe it was part of their DNA.

William looked past Fiona toward the crowd of partygoers. His eyes squinted as though trying to locate Lady Roselyn. "You know your sister. At times, crowds make her uncomfortable. I'm sure she's nestled into a corner with a good romance novel." He tipped his hat. "I'd best check on the horses, but I'll return as soon as I can." He patted Fiona on the arm. "Don't look so worried. Things will work out, you'll see."

"But not always the way we expect."

He chuckled. "Well, there is that."

She stood a moment longer at the door as William disappeared into the night. She'd just settled down by the table to wait when the door banged open, sending frigid air into the alcove.

The music played on, and no one seemed aware of the intrusion. Liam entered with a dark expression, looking every inch the role he'd been asked to play. His dark hair was tied at the nape of his neck, and he looked like he'd been battling dragons. If she were the swooning type, she'd have made a fool of herself and rushed into his arms. As it was, she had to concentrate on staying seated. On his heels was the representative from the matchmaker council, Andrew Campbell.

Like Liam, Andrew was dressed as a highwayman, but his clothes were ill-fitted on his lean frame, as though he'd rented them for a fantasy convention.

"I told you to stop following me," Liam shot back over his shoulder at the man.

Andrew whipped off his hat. Water dripped from the broad brim and pooled on the wood floor. "For the hundredth time, I've told you it's my job to review your clients and their assignments. There have been too many mistakes, and the council is considering making a few changes. The council wants the adventures safe for everyone."

"I need a drink." Liam tore off his cape and tossed it over the chair near Fiona. The expression in his eyes reminded her of storm clouds.

Fiona pushed the glass of ale on the table in his direction. Liam caught the movement, as she knew he would, and crossed over toward her. He hesitated for a moment while he held her gaze, then sat down, draining half the drink in one gulp.

"Just so you know," Andrew said, "I'm planning on returning to Paris to make sure Emma and Björn make the rendezvous location in time."

"Fine," Liam shot back.

"I'm not the enemy."

Fiona had had enough. "Stop it, the both of you. We are all on the same side, and despite you saying so to the contrary," she said, nodding at Andrew, "you *are* behaving like our enemy. You attack one of us and it is like you are attacking us all."

Andrew slapped his hat against his thigh. "If you'll excuse me, I'm going to find the bar."

Fiona waited a few seconds to make sure Andrew was far enough away, then said, "How did it really go?"

Liam took another drink. "Emma is a lot tougher than she looks. That's the good news, but I think Björn was having trouble finding us, so I veered off script to draw his attention. The only thing I could think of was to discharge my pistol."

Fiona leaned toward him. "That weapon is an antique. It might have blown up in your face."

He nodded with a grin. "Don't think that didn't cross my mind. But it had to be done. I had to get Björn's attention." He moved his jaw back and forth, rubbing it with his hand, and then chuckled. "That fisherman packs a solid punch. He reminds me of a freight train. If I hadn't backed off and pretended I was unconscious, he would have kept on coming. You have to admire the guy. 'Course, he thought I was a first-class jerk." Liam paused. "They both did."

She could tell how much that bothered him. His role was to play the bad guy, never the hero. "It's just a part you have to play. It's not you."

"That's the story I tell myself, as well."

She resisted the impulse to reach out to him, touch his hand, and say she was sorry he'd been hurt, sorry that he always had to be the villain. Their personal wishes and desires didn't matter. They'd both been born into this life, and like her sisters, they had specific roles to play.

She looked toward Andrew and lowered her voice. "I want you to be more careful. You take too many risks. In Scotland, you almost…"

Liam glanced across the room toward the bar where Andrew was ordering a drink, then turned back to Fiona. "I'm more worried that Andrew will find out how we feel about each other."

"I don't care a fig if he finds out. I'd think the council would be happy to learn that we love each other."

Liam's eyes crinkled at the corners. "You just admitted you love me. That's a first."

"Of course I love you, you infuriating lump. You're missing the point. The council insists on an arranged marriage with the misguided belief that if a couple isn't in love with each other, they can concentrate on matching other couples rather than spending time together." She stole a glance toward Andrew. "But just to be on the safe side, I don't want him to find out how we feel until after the marriage. Now, tell me why you were so angry with Andrew. Is it because he mentioned that the council intends to make changes? Are they planning on replacing us?"

Liam shook his head. "He can't replace you. You and your sisters are the only ones left with the hereditary abilities to charm new doors. No, I think there's something else he's worried about. Probably the same thing that has us all worried."

Fiona felt a chill spread over her skin as though a window had been opened. "Someone is tampering with the doors."

"Bingo."

Chapter Twenty-Seven

The chocolate was warm in Björn's mouth, and Emma's touch was feather soft as she fed him another chocolate-dipped piece of cake. Their time here had passed without a new clue as to where they'd go next, and if Björn was being honest, he didn't care. There had been a nonstop parade of customers since they'd first arrived that reminded him of the coffee houses in the United States. People met friends, their dates, or dropped by for a solitary beverage. The bustle of normalcy was comforting.

He speared another piece of cake to dunk in the warm chocolate.

"You have chocolate on your lip," Emma said, leaning over to wipe his mouth with her napkin.

She gave him a smile and reached for another piece of cake, then set it down. "I am so full. I can't believe I'm saying this, but I can't eat anymore."

He chuckled. "Your secret is safe with me. Drat. My cake dropped off my fork."

She leaned back in her chair. "We are friends, right?"

He gave up trying to fish the cake out of the chocolate and looked over at her.

"Absolutely."

"And friends can ask friends anything."

He held his breath. Waiting.

"Never mind. It's really none of my business."

It was his turn to reach for her hand. "Yes. You can ask me anything."

"Are you sure?"

He hated the sound of the uncertainty he heard in her voice. He wanted to return to the way they were when they were younger. Good news or bad, Emma was the one he told first, and it was the same for her. It was as though they knew each other's thoughts. They'd never spoken of it, but he suspected she knew as well as he did the moment their friendship had grown into something more.

How long had he been falling in love with Emma?

All his life came the swift answer.

The door opened and a crush of people flowed into the room like a tidal wave. While Claude helped the new customers find tables, a woman wearing a hat with a dark veil over her face entered in their wake. She was dressed more simply than the others in the room. A few people whispered and nodded toward her as though she was a celebrity of some sort. She kept to the shadows and passed a slip of paper to a red-haired waiter, then disappeared into a back room.

"Who do you think she is?" Emma said, peering over her shoulder in the direction the woman had vanished.

Björn shook his head. "You are amazing, Emma Grey. We're stuck back in time and instead of becoming hysterical, you're excited about the possibility of meeting someone we've only read about in history books."

He'd kept his hand on Emma's, telling himself that he'd returned to the Village for his father's sake, but that was only part of the story. He'd returned because he needed to see Emma. "You can ask me anything," he repeated.

"Stop blaming yourself for your brother's death," she said in a rush.

"How is it that you know me so well?"

She put her other hand on top of his. "We're friends." She let her words fill the space between them. "Your brother's death was not your fault."

"I should have been able to save Sven from drowning," Björn said.

"Jorvy told me that the crew said you dived in after him, that the storm was relentless, and the waves almost swamped the ship and sank it. They managed to pull you both out, but only you survived."

Björn slipped his hands from her grasp and leaned back in his chair, rubbing them over his head. "I'm a strong swimmer. I should have been able to save him."

"If you couldn't, no one could. You have to forgive yourself."

"Jorvy said the same thing. It's not that easy. Forgiveness is not a switch you can turn off and on. You don't wake up one morning and discover that the guilt was washed from your soul. And what about you? You worry that if you had helped your mother with the errands the day she died, she'd still be alive. I don't know if there is a grand design that governs our lives, or if each one of us has a predetermined destiny, or if everything is one big jumble of disconnected events that once in a blue moon resemble a pattern. Some days I believe in all of it and other days...none of it. Over the past year, I had a lot of time to think, and one thing became crystal clear. The people we love are in our lives for a reason, and I don't believe that's random or just luck."

Björn turned away for a moment, taken off guard by the rush of emotions that hit him in the gut and the realization that Emma was his anchor and the one person who kept him from breaking apart on the rocks.

When he turned back, a peace, like a ray of sunshine, warmed him to his core. "I learned something else after my mother and brother died. We can't control how long those we love are in our lives. What we can control is that we let them know how we feel when they are with us."

"I miss her," Emma said, looking down at her clenched hands. "When you were away, did you discover a strategy to make the hurt we feel go away?"

Björn wiped a tear from Emma's cheek. "It helps to remember the good times and the laughter. For example, did you know that my brother hated the taste of fish? All fish, in fact, no matter how our mother tried to disguise the taste with heaping spoonsful of sauce."

She sniffled and shook her head.

He grinned. "It was our family's dark secret. Imagine generations of fishermen, all tracing their history back to the Vikings, and discovering one of them can't stand the taste of fish. My father made our brother vow he'd never mention it to anyone."

Emma wiped her face with the back of her hand and smiled. "What did your brother eat when you went fishing for months on end?"

"Oatmeal. Gallons and gallons of oatmeal."

The waiter with red hair handed Emma a slip of paper. She knew without question that it was the one the woman in the veil had handed him.

"What does the note say?" Björn said.

"It's a drawing of this room, with arrows pointing in the direction the woman in the veil left a little while ago. Do you think it's a clue?"

Suddenly, the street door banged open, letting in a blast of cold air. Instead of customers entering the chocolate shop, a man stood in the doorway as though he couldn't cross the threshold. The man was draped in shadows: his wide-brimmed hat was pulled down low and obscured his identity as his dark cape billowed out behind him in the wind.

The man focused on Björn and shouted, "Run!"

One minute the highwayman had been standing in the doorway, and the next he'd vanished, leaving just the one word ringing in Björn's ears.

Run!

Björn reached for Emma's hand and turned to leave, but Claude blocked their path.

He held a carafe of drinking chocolate. His voice was an octave higher than normal and dripped with sugar. "You can't leave yet, *mademoiselle et monsieur*. I've made my specialty."

"Thank you, but we have to leave." Björn said, edging around Claude. Björn looked over toward the doorway, making sure the highwayman hadn't reappeared. Odd. It was as though the highwayman had been trying to warn them.

Claude followed the direction of Björn's gaze. "*Oh, mon dieu*. Is something wrong?"

"We've stayed here too long." Björn tightened his grip on Emma's hand and started back in the direction she'd indicated.

"You cannot leave," Claude insisted, setting the

carafe on the table. "These are troubling times." His voice lost its sugar coating. "You must stay. I insist."

When Claude reached for Emma's arm, Björn stood in his way. "We're leaving."

"No, you are not," Claude said, pulling a pistol from his waistcoat.

For the second time that day, Björn punched a man in the jaw.

Chapter Twenty-Eight

Clutching the map the waiter had given her, Emma raced beside Björn into the room at the back of the chocolate shop where she'd seen the woman in the veil disappear. Bookshelves rose to the ceiling in every direction. Emma examined the map closer. "If I'm reading this correctly, there is a hidden passageway behind one of these bookshelves." She raised her head to look over at Björn. "Do you think Claude followed us?"

"He'll be unconscious for a little while at least. I hit him pretty hard." Björn lifted a lantern he'd grabbed on his way out of the chocolate shop. The light illuminated the bank of bookcases that stretched the length of the walls. "What are we looking for, exactly?"

Emma held the map near the lantern. "There's a circle around a red book. That must mean something."

"Red book it is, then." He lifted the lantern higher as he searched the shelves. It illuminated a red leather book, but instead of taking the book off the shelf, he pulled it toward him a few inches. There was a click, and a section of the bookshelf moved inward.

An invitation.

"We could go back," Björn said. "This could lead straight into a trap."

Emma fingered the slip of paper between her fingers. "We were given this map for a reason. You said yourself that Bridget told you we'd receive clues. I'm game if you are."

Björn grinned. "This is like the time in fifth grade when we stayed out all night and searched the abandoned house looking for ghosts."

"We were grounded for a week."

Björn chuckled. "It was worth it."

"Yes, it was." Emma placed her hand on Björn's shoulder. "Lead the way."

Chapter Twenty-Nine

The light from the lantern candle's flames flickered off the walls as Emma and Björn reached the bottom of a spiral staircase. At the base of the stairs was a curved wooden door.

A square peephole slid open and the outline of a person's face filled the space. "You are expected," came a gravelly voice as the door opened.

The room was ablaze with light and conversation, and women outnumbered the men. Small groups discussed a wide range of topics from mathematics, philosophy, science, and literature to the current state of politics in France. Had the nobility grown too rich? The clergy too powerful? Would there be a revolution? Snippets of conversation danced around the room with less serious consequences, ranging from the clothes worn by Marie Antoinette at the gaming tables to her latest lover.

A waiter seemed to materialize out of thin air, handing Emma and Björn demitasse cups of drinking chocolate, only to disappear back into the crowd.

Emma leaned over to whisper to Björn, "Do you see the woman in the veil?"

"Not so far. What is this place?"

"I believe it's called a literary salon. In the United States, some people believe the word 'feminism' is a modern term, but it has deep roots in Europe, particularly in England and France. In salons like this one, women could discuss their views on a wide range of subjects, without fear of judgment or reprisal. When my mother and I visited Paris, we spent the day learning that some of these women not only spoke out for reform but fought alongside men in the French Revolution. And now we have the chance to hear them first hand. Do you think we'll find another clue here?"

"The clue might not be a what but a who," Björn said. "We should split up and look around."

Emma nodded as Björn disappeared into the crowd. She headed in the opposite direction, toward a small group nestled near a fireplace, all the while attempting to tamp down her excitement. Her apprehension had been replaced by curiosity.

The chocolate shop taste-testing had been fun, but it paled in comparison to a chance to meet women she'd only read about. Emma paused a moment, trying to decide which group to join. On her left, a woman was reading from a manuscript to a group of men and women. Another group was headed by a woman who debated French law as it applied to women's and children's rights. A third group discussed the women who had used code names, or what the French called *noms de guerre*, like Amazon or Princess to disguise their identity.

Emma made her way to a circle of people near the fireplace. A famous newspaper, *Journal des Dames*, written mostly by female journalists, lay on a table near two women engaged in a lively debate over the topic of Marie Antoinette. Beside the newspaper was a hat with a black veil attached.

Emma's pulse quickened as she moved closer

toward the two women.

"The queen is not what she appears," said the woman who had her back turned toward Emma. "Charlotte, are you aware that Marie's favorite painter is the artist Louise-Elisabeth Vigée-Lebrun?"

"Who in Paris is not? Perhaps the queen admires Louise-Elisabeth because she knows the woman will not paint her flaws."

"Perhaps. Certainly, royal painters are aware their artistic freedoms are limited and subject to the whims of their benefactors," the woman with her back to Emma defended. "I believe there is more to the story. Marie and Louise-Elizabeth are the same age, and it is said that Louise-Elisabeth considers the Queen to have great dignity and grace. They respect each other. To employ a female painter may be only a little rebellion, but make no mistake, it is a rebellion, nonetheless." She took a sip of drinking chocolate and continued, "A woman, even a queen, is considered little more than a breeder and a man's ignorant plaything. Marie has little power in these times." The woman patted the newspaper resting on the table beside her. "In elevating Louise-Elizabeth, our queen is making a statement, very much in accord with the female journalist in this paper. Talent is not exclusively a male trait. Never forget. It takes real courage to speak out."

Emma was mesmerized by the conversation between these two women. History had come to life. She edged closer, still unable to see the woman who's back was turned away, but the voice sounded familiar.

"The Queen could fight for us and for our rights," Charlotte said. Her voice rose in passion. "Or write an editorial for my newspaper."

"And what would you have her do? Speak out and risk losing her head?"

"Nothing will happen to Marie," Charlotte continued. "Only women of low birth are burned at the stake or dragged out of their homes and murdered. She changes her gowns every hour, orders the gardens outside her quarters dug up and replanted once a month, drinks from goblets shaped like her breasts, and eats desserts made from spun gold, while we starve."

"The tales of the Queen and her court become more fantastical with each retelling of the story. The truth lies somewhere in between."

"I agree," Emma blurted.

The woman named Charlotte raised her head and glanced in Emma's direction. "Well said, newcomer." She paused as her gaze traveled over Emma. "Welcome to our salon. Here you are free to express your opinions without fear of reprisal. Tell us more of your opinion of our Queen."

Emma moistened her dry lips. "I think Marie has been misunderstood. She was married at a young age and brought to France, where her most important duty was to look pretty and have children. She was an educated woman. Even if she had tried to influence her husband for change, she would have been ignored. It has to have been frustrating for her."

The woman whose back had been toward Emma turned and smiled. "I knew there was something about you that I liked. You know your history."

"Lady Roselyn!" Emma glanced over at the hat and veil and then back toward Lady Roselyn. "You gave the waiter the map. But that means you also time…"

Lady Roselyn held a finger to her lips to silence

Emma, and she began the introductions. "Emma, I would like to introduce you to my good friend Charlotte Corday. Charlotte, may I present Emma. She has traveled a long distance to visit your wonderful city."

"A friend of yours is indeed a friend of mine," Charlotte said, opening a lace fan with a snap.

"*Ma chére*," Lady Roselyn said, "would you mind giving us a little privacy?"

Charlotte bent and kissed Lady Roselyn on both cheeks, then smiled. "Sometimes I think you have more secrets than I do. In this case, it gives me the excuse to introduce myself to the English woman who just arrived with her latest lover. She's the writer, Mary Wollstonecraft. They say she is writing a book entitled *The Vindication on the Rights of Women*. Most interesting. I'm told you and Mary Wollstonecraft are long-time acquaintances."

Lady Roselyn waved away the comment. "An exaggeration. We've met but briefly, and that was some time ago. But be sure to let her know I'm here." When Charlotte left to join another group of women, Lady Roselyn motioned for Emma to join her. "Charlotte, although in favor of a revolution, wants a more peaceful solution. It's a pity few will listen to her, and I'm saddened at the choices she will make. But that is a discussion for another day. We must be very careful. These people must never know we are from the future."

Emma glanced over at Charlotte, who was joining Mary Wollstonecraft's group. Mary had been the woman reading from her manuscript earlier. "Mary Wollstonecraft. That name is familiar. Wasn't she the mother of Mary Shelley?"

"Very good. Yes, you know your history.

Unfortunately, Mary died giving birth to her daughter. She would have been very proud that her daughter went on to write *Frankenstein*." Lady Roselyn reached for Emma's hands. "This adventure for you and Björn has not gone as I'd planned, but this century is exciting and the women inspiring. I'm surprised, however, that you left the chocolate house so soon."

Emma leaned forward. "We didn't have a choice. First someone dressed like the highwayman who'd attacked my coach shouted for us to run, and then one of our waiters pointed a gun at us."

Lady Roselyn's gaze widened as she glanced around the room, as though fearful someone might burst in on them. "A highwayman, you say? But that must mean…? What did the waiter look like?"

"Thin face, wore gloves, dressed in red and purple."

"It's worse than I thought. Find Björn. We need to leave. Immediately."

Chapter Thirty

Emma and Björn followed Lady Roselyn through a maze of corridors until they reached the street level. After the brightness of the literary salon, it took a moment for Emma's eyes to adjust to the darkness.

The clatter of horse's hooves on cobblestones and the shouts of men came from a short distance away. With each second that passed the noise intensified.

"Come with me," Lady Roselyn said, pulling the hood of her cape over her head.

The streets narrowed. Shadows bunched in corners or elongated like fingers reaching out to grab the innocent and pull them into a dark abyss. After the friendly atmosphere of the chocolate shop and the salon, this was a rude awakening. It was a stark reminder of not only where Emma had traveled but, more importantly, when.

Lady Roselyn guided Emma and Björn to a stone building. The arched double doors were twice Björn's height and were overlaid with moldings and green swirls. In the center of each door was the raised image of a vase that held pink rosebuds. The flowers looked like they belonged on one of Emma's wedding cakes. On a plaque above the entrance, written in gold leaf, were the French words, *Mille sept cent quatre-vingt-neuf*, which Emma knew was the year: seventeen hundred eighty-nine. The same year the French

Revolution began in earnest.

Emma rubbed her arms against a sudden chill. She couldn't remember the exact date Paris had erupted in chaos.

"What's wrong?" Björn said.

Emma shook her head. "I'm okay."

The door before them opened, and a man dressed in formal attire greeted them with a smile. He had changed his clothes, but the carrot-red hair was as good as a calling card. He was the waiter who'd handed Emma the map. His eyes seemed to warm as he gazed at Lady Roselyn. "*Bonsoir*. It is a pleasure to see you again so soon."

"*Merci*, Barnard. I entrust Emma and Björn into your care. Please watch over them for me."

He winked. "Have I ever failed you?"

Lady Roselyn's face flushed as she kissed Barnard on both cheeks, then stepped back. She appeared hesitant, as though debating whether to stay. Within seconds, whatever internal battle she'd waged appeared over. She lifted her chin, her voice once again formal as she turned toward Emma and Björn. "Have fun, my darlings. There is a door inside that will guide you back to the Matchmaker Café, but it won't open until the stroke of midnight. I must attend to another couple in need of my assistance. Until then, enjoy the ball and the magic that Paris has to offer."

Bernard opened the door wider and gave a slight bow.

Light, music, and warmth rushed toward Björn in equal measures, and Emma had the distinct impression that attending the party was not an option.

Chapter Thirty-One

If the Matchmaker Café looked like the inside of a faceted ruby, Marie's ballroom was a pastry chef's inspiration. Emma slipped her arm around Björn's as they moved out of the way of arriving guests. Chandeliers, frosted with gold and polished silver, hung from the ceiling and were reflected in the mirrors that lined the walls of the room. Guests gathered in groups like clusters of spring bouquets. An orchestra tuned their instruments, while waiters carried platters of champagne and a variety of finger foods.

The people crowding the room wore thick layers of makeup and were dressed so elaborately they didn't look real. They spoke in French, Italian, and German, used hand gestures to emphasize a point, kissed each other on both cheeks in greeting, or checked out their appearance in the wall-to-wall mirrors.

"*Bonjour, mes amis,*" a woman said in lyrical French as she drew near Emma.

All conversations in the room ceased as though a switch had been turned off. The woman wore a candy-pink-and-cream gown and a wig that looked like a triple scoop of vanilla ice cream dusted with sprinkles. Peeking out from under the hem of her gown were shoes studded with crystals. The man walking beside her carried himself like a soldier. He wore a silk jacket, matching fitted pants that ended at the knees, and silk hose, all in the same shades as the woman's gown.

The woman stopped in front of Emma and made a delicate gesture with her hand. Immediately, someone appeared and handed Emma and Björn white velvet masks outlined in rhinestones. "*Bienvenue*," the woman announced. With her hand at the base of her tall wig to keep it from tipping, she continued in a voice as delicate as spun silk. "Welcome, American friends. We heard you had arrived. I am Marie, and may I present to you my dearest friend, Axel von Fersen Gothenburg."

Axel swept his arm in a wide arc and bowed. "Welcome indeed," he said, then turned to Marie. "Their expressions remind us of the star-crossed lovers, Tristan and Isolde, don't they, my dear? Much too serious for a night such as this."

Marie snapped her fan open, examining Emma and Björn. "You have described them perfectly."

Emma tucked a strand of hair behind her ear, resisting the impulse to check a mirror, which given the number in the room was a true test of will power. Björn hadn't seemed to register Axel's comments and kept glancing over his shoulder. For her part, she wasn't sure being compared to Tristan and Isolde was a good thing, given their ending.

Did she and Björn look tragic? She didn't want to be that type of couple, the half-empty kind, for whom everything was a drama or a struggle. She wanted to be the kind of person who discovered joy in the small things, like a child's laughter, and how rain made flowers sparkle like crystals.

Her mother had enjoyed that outlook on life. When she and her mother visited Paris, they had called it their nonstop giggle fest. The smallest things would cause them to burst into laughter: small dogs carried in handbags, street mimes, or walking in the rain.

Axel leaned to whisper in Marie's ear. A pink tint the same shade as her gown added to the glow of her rouged cheeks. Her voice was a breathy whisper. "Of course, *mon amour*. Our song." She hesitated for a moment, then turned toward Emma with a thin smile. "Remember, *mes amis*, time can be a blessing or a curse. You can choose to embrace each moment, or regret that life is too short. True happiness lies in the choices you make."

Axel reached for Marie's hand, kissing her fingers, and mirroring her melancholy expression. Marie's smile blossomed. "*Mon amour*," she said and slipped one ring-clad hand into Axel's, waved farewell with the other, and stepped to the dance floor with him, where they danced around and around the room, locked in their own world.

Conversation resumed as quickly as it had stopped as people joined the couple on the dance floor or headed for refreshments. The woman's words flowed through Emma's thoughts, awakening a memory. Her mother had said something like that on their visit to Paris. But it wasn't just Marie's words that were familiar.

Björn's eyebrows were drawn together. "Is something wrong?"

Emma shrugged. "I know this sounds crazy, but that woman looks exactly like a portrait of Marie Antoinette my mother and I noticed in the Palace of Versailles. Is it possible that Lady Roselyn arranged an invitation to one of Marie's famous parties?"

"If I've learned anything in the last few hours, it's

that anything is possible." The corner of Björn's mouth edged up in a smile. "That's the first time I've ever heard you talk about your visit here with your mother."

Emma moved closer to Björn as guests continued to arrive. He was right. She'd kept those memories locked away as though speaking about them would expose her to more pain. But talking about her mother just now had created the opposite effect, and she wanted more. Emma smiled at the realization.

"My mom and I took one of those guided tours at the Palace of Versailles, and she made it come alive. At first the guide only wanted to point out the tapestries, portraits, statues, and furniture, but that all changed when my mother started asking questions. She would ask about Marie Antoinette's favorite desserts, if it were true that she liked to gamble, or how often she'd disguised herself so that she could sneak into Paris and dance until dawn."

Björn put his arm around Emma's waist. "And don't forget all the cookies your mother baked for my lunches or the time she helped my mother bake cupcakes for my scout troop. Your mother was amazing."

Emma loved that he had beautiful memories of her mom. It was something else they shared. She slipped her hand into his and scanned the dance floor. The music beckoned as couples twirled past her.

Björn held out his hand toward Emma.

She slipped her hands into the folds of her gown. Ever since prom, she'd dreamed of the moment when he'd ask her to dance. She'd accept. He'd hold her in his arms. She'd believe they had a future. She could feel the walls shooting up around her. She shook her head. "The dance steps look too difficult."

He reached for her hands. "I missed my opportunity in high school to dance with the most beautiful girl at the prom, and I'm not doing that again. Besides, everyone is too busy looking at themselves in the mirror to notice us." He grinned. "One more thing: I don't care if everyone is wearing a mask, I'm not wearing one." He tossed it on a tray as a waiter passed by.

He was right. Everyone wore masks, each one more elaborate than the last, and decorated with feathers, ribbons, and multi-colored crystals. The masks weren't so much a fashion accessory as a way of hiding a person's identity. She thought back to Axel's comment comparing her and Björn to Tristan and Isolde. That had bothered her. She didn't want to be part of a tragic anything.

"Axel thought we reminded him of the lovers Tristan and Isolde," she said.

Björn's eyebrows knitted together. "I don't remember him saying that. My thoughts were somewhere else, but didn't those two end up the same way as Romeo and Juliet?"

Emma nodded, a little surprised he knew about them. "It was forbidden for Tristan and Isolde to be together, and both died rather than live without each other."

A muscle flexed along the side of his jaw. "How is that romantic?"

She handed the waiter her mask and took Björn's hand. "People think it was romantic because they defied their families so they could be together in death. Sometimes it's just not meant to be."

"I don't believe that. They gave up too easily. They should have figured a way to work things out," he said as they headed toward the dance floor.

"It wasn't that simple," Emma pressed, wondering why Björn had taken this topic so seriously. "In the case of Romeo and Juliet, there were family expectations and responsibilities. They couldn't just run away."

His expression clouded over as he swept her onto the dance floor and around the room. Their reflection in the mirrors was a blaze of color.

He was turning her so fast she had to hold onto his shoulders.

"Tristan and Isolde were more like Lancelot and Guinevere," she continued. "Both Isolde and Guinevere were married to kings. They were more living ornaments than true partners. There is a raging debate, even to this day, as to whether the kings they'd married loved them or were just attracted to their beauty. Both women fell in love with men who at least appeared to love them for themselves, but how could they have known for sure? The women felt trapped in loveless marriages."

"You are an expert on the past, but the people in the present you keep at a distance." He spun her around the dance floor at a frantic pace.

She felt as dizzy as a spinning top as she held onto him. Was what he said true? Did she keep everyone at a distance?

He stopped suddenly in the middle of the dance floor and ran his hands through his hair. "And then there's you and me. What's up with us? Every time one of us tries to move past 'just friends,' the other throws a wrench into the works, or sets up impossible road blocks, or flat out runs away. I admit, I'm guilty of all three. But if two people want to be together, they should be together. It shouldn't be complicated."

Björn spun around and headed toward a bank of doors on the far side of the room. As she watched Björn walk into an adjacent room without her, Emma felt as though he took all the air with him. Was he right?

She stood alone in the middle of the dance floor. Dancers swirled around her in a blur of color and sound. Emma called many of the shop owners in the Village her friends, except the truth was that she didn't know anything about most of them. Did Mr. Rigby have children? Were the twins homeschooled? Most of all, she kept Björn at a distance.

She knew about Daisy only because she talked nonstop about her life, not because Emma asked questions. In return, Emma offered crumbs of information about herself, or how much she missed her mother. Revealing too much made her feel vulnerable. The shell around her heart kept her safe, and on and on. She'd traveled on this rationalization train ever since her mother's death. That way of thinking was an illusion, a trick of smoke and mirrors that she had used to convince herself that she was connected to the world. Instead of keeping her safe, it had ensured her isolation. And Björn was right. Every time they got close, one of them did something to blow it up.

She wrapped her arms around her waist as she tried to take deep, even breaths. Each one felt labored.

Marie and Axel danced around her, the picture of a candy lover's dream, all pink icing and sugar-coated smiles. On closer examination, their expressions looked forced, and their laughter sounded brittle, as though one false step and the illusion they'd created would shatter. Was that the type of life Emma had also created for herself? Marie had said that true happiness lay in the choices you make. But the choices should be your choices, not the ones others made for you.

Emma wanted everyone to believe that her life was perfect. That she was keeping her mother's bakery alive and thus her mother's memory with it. But she was disconnected from everything around her, clinging to the illusion that the only thing that mattered was her mother's dream. She had a feeling that the only person she was fooling was herself. What were her dreams? What did she want?

Keep it simple, came the answer. You know the answer. You've always known.

Taking a deep breath, she rushed after Björn.

Chapter Thirty-Two

Emma followed Björn into a room with tall windows and long tables where desserts were displayed on every available surface like wildflowers over a sugar-coated meadow. There were flowers made from marzipan, macaroon cookies in every shade of the rainbow, and tiered cakes with leaves she suspected were made from sheets of real gold.

He stood with his back toward her, but turned his head to the side as she entered. "I'm sorry. That was a jerk thing to say."

"You were being honest. We push each other away."

He turned and the passion in his eyes took her breath away. Her heart beat in response. "My dad was right. I think I waited too long."

"My mother said it's never too late. I think she was talking about mastering the perfect chocolate soufflé, but it's good advice."

His gaze heated. She tucked a hair behind her ear as her skin flushed. There were so many things she wanted to say, so many things she wished Björn would say. She needed a way to fill the silence. When she baked, everything came into focus, and if ever she needed to think clearly, it was now. "I should make you a cake. What flavor do you want? Chocolate or vanilla?"

His eyebrow lifted in the way that made butterflies take off in her stomach. "That's really not necessary."

"I disagree. I haven't made you a cake in a very long time, so it's long overdue. Why did you ask me to stop making them in the first place?"

"My birthday is the same day as Valentine's. You covered my cakes with hearts, naked cupids, and pink flowers. Have you any idea how much grief my brothers gave me?"

She smothered a smile. His expression reminded her of when they had been children. He'd always accepted whatever she made, but she could tell he would have liked something less girly. "That's not entirely true. One year you asked me to decorate your cake with horses and, as I remember, I did as you asked."

He lifted that wonderful eyebrow again. "I expected cowboys, wild mustangs, maybe spaceships; you decorated my cake with unicorns and rainbows."

She pressed her lips together to smother a laugh. "You never said a word."

"A man will endure most anything for the woman he…" Björn sucked in his breath. "What are we doing? You have a boyfriend."

"I have a confession to make. I don't have a boyfriend."

"What about the flowers?"

"I sent them to myself."

"The picture?"

She grimaced. "The picture came with the frame. Daisy often said he reminded her of a romance novel's cover model."

He turned away, trying to hide a laugh. When he

turned back, he was more serious. "Why did you do all of this?"

"I wanted to make you jealous."

He shook his head, smiling. "It worked," he said.

"Are you kidding me? You didn't say a word."

"What did you expect me to do? Confess my undying love for you?"

"Yes. That would be a great start. Are you aware most of the guys I dated were there only to make you jealous?"

"And the others?"

"You are so infuriating. I tell you I only dated to make you jealous and you focus on the one or two guys I might have liked. Sometimes you make me want to…want to…"

"Throw another pie in my face?"

"Yes…I mean…no."

He smiled, brushing a stray curl from her forehead. "You should probably make me a cake."

"Yes," she stammered. "That's a good idea," she said in a rush. "I can make a completely un-Valentine's Day birthday cake." She walked around the room, looking for a distraction.

None seemed fit for Björn's birthday cake. She could scrape some of the frosting off one of the cakes and add a simple design. With a clear plan in mind, she chose a chocolate cake with the least decoration. She then reached for a flat metal spatula and began carefully shaving off the thick buttercream frosting.

Björn kissed her neck.

Her knees buckled. The only thing preventing her from falling to the floor in a puddle was his arm around her waist. How long had she wanted him to kiss her in that exact spot? It felt as though she'd always fantasized about this moment. Once she'd even tried to do something about it. They had been in their twenties, and he'd returned from Alaska for the holidays, and she had been determined to get his attention. That winter had been particularly cold and brutal, but she'd dressed in short skirts and barely-there tops to get his attention. The only thing she'd accomplished had been contracting a cold that had made her nose as red and bulbous as a circus clown's.

She leaned against his chest and tilted her head to the side, savoring the moment as his mouth traced a path of kisses over her bare shoulders. A shiver of pleasure coated her skin in a delicious warmth. This was heaven.

The door to the small room was flung open, letting in a chattering collection of waiters that reminded Emma of wide-eyed hens at feeding time, led by a rooster.

Startled, she swung toward the waiters, and in the process she whacked Björn across the shoulder with the spatula. Great globs of frosting sprayed over his face and jacket. Frantically, she grabbed a linen towel from a waiter's arm to clean off Björn's clothes.

The waiter, the one who reminded Emma of a rooster, noticed Emma and Björn for the first time and gave an elaborate bow of apology. "*Pardonnez-moi*," he said, then straightened, clapping his hands toward the hens, shouting for them to hurry. In a flurry of activity, trays were loaded with desserts from the tables in assembly-line fashion, and then everyone paraded back out through the open door. The head waiter bowed, apologizing again for the intrusion, and as he closed the door, he said something that sounded a lot like, "As you were."

Emma and Björn burst out laughing.

Still chuckling, Björn wiped frosting off his face with the towel Emma had provided and then wiped at the frosting on his jacket. "They spoiled my best move."

Emma took the towel from him. "Let me help you. You're rubbing the frosting into the cloth." She kept her head down, wanting to keep the mood light. "That was your best move?"

"Pretty much. Now you know why I'm single."

She dabbed at the frosting that had splattered across his sleeve. She knew for an almost certainty that the reason he was single was because he wanted it that way. With his Viking good looks, most women wouldn't care if he could carry on a conversation, let alone whether he had smooth moves.

Emma reached up and used her thumb to remove frosting from the side of his mouth. "You missed a spot on your face. You're covered in pink frosting. It seems you can't get away from that color."

He took the towel from her and tossed it on the counter. "What makes you think I want to get away?"

His words brushed over her skin like a caress. She wanted to freeze this moment in time. Hold onto it. Never let it go.

Björn kissed the tip of her nose. "What are you thinking?" Although they stood only a heartbeat from each other, she could feel him pull away. "If you don't feel the same way…"

She reached up and placed her fingers over his lips. "I just can't believe this is happening, after all this time.

I never thought…"

He pulled her into his arms, his mouth warm against hers as his kiss deepened. She felt wave after wave of sensations as she gave over to his kisses…to him. The world around her spun at a dizzying rate, and yet she never had felt more rooted to the ground. This was how it had always been with Björn. But was that why she'd kept him at arm's length? She thought he was too good to be true?

Her heart thundered in her throat so hard she thought it might rise above the music in the next room. Ignore the doubts. Live in the now.

He knocked the cakes to the floor with a wide sweep of his arm, lifting her to a sitting position on the table and cupping her face with his hands.

All her fantasies, all her wild imagining of how it would feel to be in his arms, paled in comparison to the real thing. She was in the arms of the man she loved, had always loved. She never wanted this night to end.

Chapter Thirty-Three

Fiona had used the door leading to Edinburgh Castle in the sixteen hundreds, and now she didn't want to leave. She'd gone there with all the best intentions. This was the location where the matchmaking council met this month. It was also where Duncan lived. Not only had she not accomplished her goal, she had made everything worse. She'd wanted to find out if the council really intended to replace them.

She reached for the door handle that would take her from the sixteenth century back to her own time, but she had a hard time turning the knob. She didn't want to leave. No, that wasn't exactly true. She didn't want to leave…him. After her failed meeting with the council, she'd sought Duncan to see if her feelings for him were real, only to realize that he was preoccupied with battle strategy. Something about an invasion.

Occasionally, someone would bring up the irony that matchmakers were dedicated to creating love matches while being forced into marriages that were more about bloodlines and magical gifts than love. But nothing was done to change the tradition.

She glanced over her shoulder toward the castle's great hall, searching one last time. Only a few of the clan's representatives remained. Duncan was not among them.

She shook herself mentally. She was a fool. Worse.

They'd exchanged a few words, barely enough to make up a complete sentence. There were no lingering glances, no touching, no stolen kisses, and yet she couldn't stop thinking about him. Could she marry Liam with unresolved feelings for Duncan? And what if what she was feeling for Duncan wasn't real? What if it was more rebellion against an arranged marriage than love?

"Stop it," she said under her breath. "You're betrothed to Liam." She gave herself another mental shake and took a deep breath to prepare for the journey from this time to her own.

Fiona opened the door and stepped into the void between times.

To keep her mind occupied, she tried to identify the moment the air currents shifted from ice cold to tropical warmth, or to distinguish the chaos of lights, or the jumble of music. Recently when she traveled, sights and sounds were compressed as though she were hearing them and experiencing them all at once. It was like someone had added a packet of blue glitter to a jar filled with water and then shaken the jar.

"Stop." She shut her eyes and pressed her hands against her ears, trying to will the sights and sounds to settle down. The more often she used the doors, the more vivid her experiences. That couldn't be good.

For first time travelers, the journey felt as though it were measured in seconds, all mist and shadows, a blink and it was over. The first dozen times or so it had been like that for her as well. Now it was like she was a passenger in a car driving through rush hour traffic in New York City. The assault on the senses was intense, and she could hardly wait for it to be over.

The door to the Matchmaker Café opened with a whoosh of hot air. Fiona held onto the door jamb to get her balance.

"Where have you been?" Bridget stood with her arms crossed over her chest, her foot tapping out her frustration.

"Not now."

Bridget arched an eyebrow. "So it's true."

Fiona closed the door and locked it, keeping her back turned. Her older sister had inherited their mother's ability to intuit a person's secrets. She didn't want to share her fear that they might all be replaced. If her suspicion turned out false, she would have worried her sisters unnecessarily. "There was a clan meeting," Fiona said, sticking to the truth.

"Until recently, you considered them a waste of time." Bridget paused. "What is his name?"

Fiona's mind raced out of control. "It's not what you think."

"What I think is that you've lost your mind. What is his name?" Bridget repeated.

Fiona stepped back. It was useless to deny it. "Duncan, but I didn't go back to be with him." She hesitated, deciding to tell Bridget at least part of what she'd asked the council. "I went back to try and convince the council to delay my marriage to Liam while I sort out my feelings."

"You're lucky you're still breathing. What did they say?"

"Instead of a Christmas wedding, they said Liam and I are to be wed in the fall."

"We'll deal with that later. Right now, we have a bigger problem. We suspect someone is trying to sabotage the doors in Paris and thus Emma and Björn's means of returning to their own time."

Chapter Thirty-Four

Emma stretched and yawned. She was having such a lovely dream. Paris in the moonlight. The sound of fireworks in the distance, and she and Björn drifting along the Seine River. Where she lay was a little uncomfortable, but she was with Björn, and he'd kissed her. She sighed, still basking in the afterglow of his kisses.

Kiss, she mused. Such a simple word that evoked so many layers. There were the innocent kisses between friends or the ones the French did in greeting. When she returned to her home, she'd create a special recipe in homage to the kiss. Something along the lines of tiramisu, with its eight to ten ingredients, or Julia Child's Le Marquis, a chocolate sponge cake filled with buttercream and covered with chocolate-butter icing or a sprinkling of powdered sugar.

A wave rocked their boat, so she snuggled deeper into the warmth of Björn's embrace. She didn't want to wake up. She clung to the threads of her dream, halfway between the sleep world and the waking world.

The sisters had created such an enchanting fantasy that it was no surprise it had continued into her dreams. She'd be sure to congratulate them when she returned. The Valentine's Day Ball in make-believe Paris had felt like it was taking place in the eighteenth century. Even the desserts had been authentic.

A nagging inner voice suggested that what she'd experienced was real. Where had that idea come from? She shooed the words aside. Time travel happened only in books, TV, and the movies.

A tremor rocked her awake, dissolving the image of herself and Björn along the Seine. She yawned again. Seattle earthquake, not a wave, she reasoned, as reality distanced her from her dream world. They both must have dozed off. They were in the dessert room, on the hardwood floor. Music, muffled laughter, and the hum of conversations spoken in French, German, and Italian drifted from the other side of the walls. It had been real.

She was glad they were alone. She smiled, remembering every minute of their time together. She sighed and propped her head on her hand, watching Björn sleep.

As children, she and Björn had called earthquakes hiccups, and windstorms had been farts. It had been part of their secret language. Their classmates had never understood why they burst out laughing when they heard the weather report.

His eyes opened as though he sensed her stare. His expression filled with love the moment he caught her gaze. "I remember the first time I realized I was in love with you. I'd forgotten my homework, and you offered to give me yours."

Her heart skipped a beat. He spoke of his love for her as though he'd mentioned it a thousand times before, and maybe he had. Not in words but in actions and in how he looked at her or the importance he placed on her opinion.

She snuggled closer. "You wouldn't take my homework. You said you'd rather suffer the consequences. I think that's when I knew I was falling in love with you. But it wasn't just one event. More of a collection. Most of the time I spent trying to talk myself out of how I felt, or denying how much I missed you when you were fishing in Alaska. But if I were to pick one event…"

He lifted her chin, kissing her parted lips. "You love me," he said.

She leaned into him. "Daisy will be so surprised when we get back and tell her how we feel about each other."

His mouth curved up on one side in a mischievous grin. "Trust me. No one in the Village will be surprised, least of all your best friend." His eyebrows knitted together, as he sat up, rubbing his eyes. "What time is it?"

"Who cares?" Emma said. She pulled him back down next to her, remembering how he'd defended her against the highwayman who'd tried to kidnap her. God help her, at that moment she'd felt like the damsel rescued by her very own knight in shining armor.

Then a dark cloud slammed against her. This whole experience was only a fantasy. It would end, and they would both return to their lives in the twenty-first century. Björn might stick around for a little while, but then he'd hear the call of Alaska and take off again, leaving her alone.

He kissed the tip of her nose. "Penny for your thoughts. You looked so serious suddenly."

"I was thinking about you…us." She looked away, unable to meet his gaze.

Being in Paris again had brought back so many memories of her time here with her mother. Julia

Child's goal to introduce the art of French cooking to America had inspired her mother to open her bakery in the heart of a sleepy little town outside of Seattle. But Emma felt as stuck in time in her shop, and in her relationship with Björn, as she did in this century. They got close, like right now, and then something always pulled them apart.

"This is probably not the best time for this question," she said, "but I have to ask. What are your plans when we return?" When he drew away from her, she knew he'd misunderstood. "I'm not asking if we'll get married, since it's probably too soon for that, but we just…well…" She cleared her throat. "I wanted to ask when you think you'll return to Alaska?"

He raked his hand through his hair. "The weather won't start making it possible to fish safely until the spring. What do you mean it's too soon to talk about getting married? I love you. I thought that was obvious. Don't you love me?"

"Love has never been our problem." She lay back down, staring at the ceiling painted with a mosaic of people laughing and chasing each other in a field of flowers. Every inch of this mansion was devoted to the expression of love and songs that wanted you to believe that love was all that was needed. But was it? She didn't know anymore.

"My father left for good when I was very young," she began. "When he was home, I like to think that he did his best to give my mother and me his full attention. But my mother said she always felt that he was distracted, always planning for the time when he'd leave again." Emma brushed a tear from her eyes. "I'm not asking you to give up what you love. I'm just letting you know that I need more than a part-time relationship."

White light flashed over the windows. Björn shielded his eyes with his arm as he jumped to his feet, pulling Emma with him.

"I'm sure they're just fireworks," Emma offered, painfully aware that he hadn't responded to her question. She was also aware that she'd broken the fantasy spell they'd been under. A lump caught in her throat. Better to let him know how she felt, she reasoned, refocusing on their situation.

"By the position of the moon, it's close to midnight. We have to find the door," Björn said. "That's our only way back to our own time."

Another tremor rocked the building and vibrated over the walls. Plaster rained down from the ceiling, and a vase toppled over and shattered. Emma reached out for Björn for balance. "That felt like an earthquake."

He glanced over his shoulder toward the windows, pulling her behind him. "I'm pretty sure it was cannon fire."

Her thoughts raced in a hundred different directions at once, like marbles tossed over a tile floor. "I'm sorry, did you just say cannon fire? As in, we're under attack?"

Another tremor rocked the building, and fire broke out in one of the rooms next to theirs. Screams silenced the music. Breaking glass and the sound of panic formed a backdrop to the battle cries and gunfire.

Björn grabbed Emma's hand. "We need to find that door."

Emma had to run to keep pace with Björn's long

strides as he raced through the deserted corridors until they reached the ballroom. Remnants of the party littered the floors, and glasses of champagne and half-eaten pastries were left abandoned on the tables. Everyone had left in a panic.

When Björn reached the circular entryway, he paused. "This door is covered with flowers," he said. "I'm sure there must be a Scottish thistle in there somewhere." He reached for the doorknob and turned.

The courtyard outside Marie Antoinette's ballroom blazed with lights from distant fires. Muffled shouts, dulled by distance, formed a single voice of protest. The people were angry.

"This is the wrong door," Björn announced, slamming it shut. "It leads to a courtyard and a very angry mob."

Emma's voice shook as she clenched her hands together to keep them from trembling. "The Scottish thistle will be prominent. It won't be mixed with other flowers." She didn't know how she knew; she just did.

Men pounded against the entrance and shouted, "Break down the door! Kill everyone inside!"

Chapter Thirty-Five

Björn braced his shoulder against the entrance as Emma raced to find something to help keep it closed. Emma knew Björn couldn't hold the angry crowd at bay for long. Through a bank of windows that overlooked the gardens, she could see torch lights moving toward the manor house at a steady pace. Hours ago, the gardens had been tranquil and beautiful. All that remained was a sense of dark foreboding.

Emma scanned the ballroom. Most of the furniture had been cleared away to make room for the dancers, with only a few tables and chairs placed in group settings. She grabbed the sturdiest wooden chair she could find and raced back to Björn. Outside, the men banged on the entrance, shouting obscenities. Thank goodness the door was made of thick oak panels. Even so, it vibrated against her fingers as she positioned the chair in place under the doorknob. It would be only a matter of time before they broke through.

"Good thinking," Björn said, moving away from the door. "But it won't hold them off for long. We must find the door I came through. According to Bridget, it automatically opens at midnight."

Emma looked around. Not a clock in sight. She knew when she left the café it had been close to seven o'clock, and with all that had happened, she'd lost track of time. In some ways, it seemed like days had passed instead of hours. "Do you have any idea what time it is?"

Björn nodded. "My father insisted I learn two things before he'd let me fish without him in the ocean. The first was to swim, and the second to navigate by reading the sky. I caught a glimpse before I slammed the door shut. By the moon's position, we have a little under an hour before midnight. We can hope Bridget was wrong and the door is already unlocked."

She nodded, following his gaze. She'd never seen so many doors. Behind one of them was their way home. Would they have enough time to find the right one?

"We'll split up," Emma decided.

He pulled her in for a quick kiss before releasing her. "You're amazing. You're as calm as a seal sunning herself on a rock."

She returned a quick kiss of her own, basking in her own version of sunshine: his smile. She winked. "I do my best work under pressure."

His laughter blocked out the muffled chants of the mob for a moment. "Me too. That's something else that we share. You take one side, and I'll take the other," he said as he moved to the opposite side of the entry. Once he was in place, he shouted over his shoulder, "What does this flower on the Matchmaker Café logo look like?"

"It's called a Scottish thistle," Emma answered, raising her voice over the noise of the pounding outside. "And looks like the top of a broom that was spray painted purple."

He gave a silent nod and turned toward a set of paneled doors. She set to work as well. The first door she came to had raised panels with elaborate swirls. Not a thistle in sight. She moved on to the next one.

Björn had spoken about the things they had in common in a matter-of-fact way, as though he'd been considering them for a long time. She, on the other hand, had held the connections they shared at a distance, afraid to examine them too closely. Afraid of what they might mean. Her fallback excuse was that she didn't have time.

It was during Emma's trip to Paris that her mother had decided to redecorate their bakery with a French theme. When her mother died, Emma was so busy keeping alive her mother's dream of creating the perfect French bakery in the Northwest that she had neglected to pursue her own dream. She knew why she'd chosen the door marked Paris at the Matchmaker Café earlier this evening. She had been searching for answers.

"Any luck?" Björn shouted.

It took her a moment to realize he was speaking about the door, not her mother. She shook her head, cleared her jumbled thoughts, and refocused.

The banging grew louder and sounded like the men outside were using some sort of battering ram to break down the door. Wood split under the pressure. Voices grew louder.

Björn shot her a glance. He wasn't any closer to finding the flower than she was. His unspoken message was clear. They were running out of time.

She hurried to the next set of doors, giving them a once-over before moving on to the next. The door was arched, painted pink and had... She paused, glancing back toward the door she'd just examined. Raised panels and swirl-like designs. The same as all the others, except in the center of each swirl was a tiny Scottish thistle. The image was so small she'd missed it on the first examination.

"I found it," Emma shouted.

Björn crossed the entry toward her just as the battering ram broke through a panel in the door. Men drew the giant timber back for another assault.

Her pulse racing, Emma reached for the knob, then hesitated. "When we open the door, we should walk into the Matchmaker Café. Right?"

"Or the streets of Paris and an angry mob of French revolutionists."

"We could hide," Emma said. "Wait for someone to rescue us. This place is enormous."

"I considered that, but the men outside are carrying torches. My guess is that if they can't find us, they'll burn this place to the ground…with us in it."

"Happy thought," Emma said sarcastically.

Björn gave a sharp nod as Emma turned the knob.

Locked.

Emma's gaze tore toward Björn's.

A muscle tightened along his jawline. "I was hoping the midnight deadline was more of a suggestion, like train schedules in Italy."

"Or maybe this isn't the right door."

"There is that."

"I have another idea," Emma said. "You're right. We can't stay here. If we hurry, we might be able to make it to the door I used when I first arrived. It was under a bridge along the river. I thought I was opening a door to a chocolate shop. That should have been my first clue something was wrong." She removed the last of the pins in her hair and shook it loose. All the women at Marie's party had perfectly coifed hair. If hers looked disheveled, she might be overlooked. "We'll go in disguise. Let me wear your jacket. This dress is like a beacon that screams nobility. We'll sneak out through the gardens and try to blend into the crowd. With all the confusion and riots we might have a chance."

Another blow shattered the wood between them and the mob. Emma and Björn ducked into an alcove as the entrance doors burst open. Keeping to the shadows, they headed toward the gardens and slipped outside.

A roar of triumph and shouts of revenge split the air. The crowd converged through the entrance like a tidal wave, destroying everything in its path. Furniture was crushed underfoot, mirrors smashed, and tapestries ripped off walls.

Crouched behind a thick hedge, Björn drew Emma beside him and whispered, "We can't use a carriage. The crowd will suspect it contains nobles trying to escape. You said the door was beneath a bridge?" When Emma nodded, he grinned. "We'll need a boat."

Chapter Thirty-Six

Paris was on fire.

Emma and Björn had reached the Seine River undetected and sought refuge beneath one of the city's numerous arched bridges. They huddled in the shadows, catching their breath as soldiers marched past them in an attempt to regain control of the city. They were losing ground. The whole population of Paris was engaged in the battle, and the streets were a war zone.

Emma and Björn's only hope of reaching the alternate rendezvous point was by boat, which presented its own problems. Every boat was either occupied, in flames, or under heavy guard. Those not already on fire were guarded. Emma and Björn weren't the only ones trying to escape the city by water.

Björn kept Emma close beside him as he glanced over his shoulder in the direction of the mansion. Smoke spiraled into the night sky. As he'd predicted, the mansion where they'd partied with Marie and Axel was engulfed in flames. Some would mourn the destruction of property without considering what had driven people to the act in the first place. Revolutions, including the American and then the French uprisings, seldom accomplished solutions to all the issues that started the war in the first place. Real change took time.

But change didn't always mean large-scale revolutions. It came in the courage of everyday life, such as changing the small things—like taking the stairs instead of the elevators—and the larger ones—like going back to school or accepting a new job. Björn took a deep breath, evaluating his own inner struggle. He'd spent months away from those he loved. He knew it wasn't just about supplying his family with their livelihood. He loved the adrenaline rush of facing the unpredictability of the open seas, and conquering his fears. Could he give that up?

"Björn, Emma," a man shouted from the river. It was William. He sat in a rowboat not far from shore. A disturbance a short distance away drew William's attention. He peered into the shadows, drew his pistol, and pulled the trigger. There was the smell of gunpowder, a muffled thud, and then silence as William edged his boat against the embankment where Björn and Emma stood. "Hurry. We haven't much time. Lady Roselyn and the others began looking for you when we discovered something had happened to your door at Marie's party. She is waiting at the alternate rendezvous at the Pont Neuf Bridge. It is the one with twelve arches. Lady Roselyn will be waiting for you there. You must reach the door before the clock strikes twelve."

Chapter Thirty-Seven

Björn pulled on the oars, guiding William's rowboat toward the Left Bank and the rendezvous at Pont Neuf Bridge. William had said he couldn't go with them, as he had to let the others know he'd found them. Björn had a suspicion that the sisters' operation was much larger than he'd first thought. He also suspected that things were not going according to plan. William was worried.

One thing was certain: the French Revolution was gaining ground. Flames from barges and the burning city reflected over the River Seine like crimson shards of glass. Björn pulled on the oars in a steady rhythm, concentrating so that each time they cut into the water they made as little sound as possible. Emma sat opposite him in silence, flinching at gunfire and the screams of fighting. Shouts of *liberté, égalité,* and *fraternité* reverberated over the water.

They'd been traveling on the Seine River for almost half an hour and had passed several bridges, but none that fit William's description. They either didn't have the right number of arches, or the bridge was lined on both sides with houses.

For the time being, the crowd was interested in controlling the city. It wouldn't be long, however, until they turned their attention to blocking anyone from using the river as an escape route.

Emma's hands gripped the bench seat until her knuckles shone white. It was the only indication that she was as worried as he was. When she realized he'd been staring at her, she gifted him with what he called her "reassuring smile." He doubted she was aware that he'd catalogued them and gauged how she felt by her smile.

The one right now was merely a lifting of the corners of her mouth. He'd first seen it after his mother had died and then again at Emma's mother's funeral. She was terrified inside but didn't want anyone to know. She also had her everyday smile that didn't quite reach her eyes, and a mischievous smile like the one he had seen on the day they skipped school so he could teach her how to fish. There were many more, but the one he kept looking for was the one he'd caught a glimpse of tonight. The one that he hadn't seen in a long, long time. The smile that shouted to the rooftops that she was happy and knew she was loved.

And then she'd asked her question. "Would you give up fishing for me?" It was like asking him to stop breathing. He knew why she'd asked. It had been the same concern his mother always had when his dad, and then her sons, had gone out fishing. Emma worried that one day he might not return.

Emma reached over and pressed her hand over his. "Are you okay?" Her features were reflected in the glow of the fires along the shoreline. Her expression was a calm harbor.

Before he could respond, gunfire erupted on a bridge they'd just passed, and one of the houses was set on fire. Emma's hands tightened on the sides of the boat.

"I wish I'd found another way to reach our rendezvous," Björn said.

"We're in this together," she said. Her voice was level and strong as she drew his gaze. "Besides, there wasn't any other way. Whatever path we took would have been fraught with danger."

The corner of his lip twitched in a smile. "Fraught?"

When they were in high school Emma had gone through a phase of trying to expand his vocabulary. She'd timed the lessons for the one place she knew he wouldn't bolt: on their way to the bus stop. He knew she hadn't wanted her best friend labeled a dumb jock, so every day she'd taught him a new vocabulary word.

"Fraught is a very good word," Emma said in defense. "It means filled with or laden with…"

"I know what it means. I was remembering that you always do that."

"Do what?"

He reached forward and tucked a strand of hair behind her ear. "When I believe that my world is falling apart, you always manage to make me smile and bring me back to what's really important."

Her eyes brightened, and then her gaze focused on the bridge coming into view. "Over there." She pointed. "I think that's the Pont Neuf Bridge."

Björn nodded agreement and rowed the boat in the direction she'd indicated. Overhead, solders guarded the bridge, and for the moment their attention was concentrated on a mob that was trying to cross to the other side. Keeping to the shadows, Björn maneuvered the boat toward the embankment. When it was close enough, he jumped to shore and helped Emma. Directly above, the disagreement between the mob and soldiers had turned more violent. Someone was pushed over the bridge, while another person was shot.

When Emma and Björn landed, Lady Roselyn rushed out of the shadows to help them. As the clock tower began its countdown to midnight, she lifted her gaze to the opposite shore and paused for a slight moment in shock. "It can't be. I thought he was dead."

Chapter Thirty-Eight

Lady Roselyn made it through the entrance to the Matchmaker Café, closely following Emma and Björn. As soon as the couple entered, Emma's friend Daisy screamed with joy and rushed over. Then it seemed everything happened at once. The music stopped, and all the couples in the room turned in her direction. Quickly, Lady Roselyn moved out of the way as Emma and Björn were rushed.

She stepped farther into the shadows as the couple was surrounded and plagued with questions. Emma and Björn kept their word and recited the story of an elaborate reenactment of the French Revolution. Lady Roselyn didn't know how long they would keep the secret, but that was the least of her worries. She was certain she'd seen her husband, or someone who looked very much like him, right before they'd entered the passageway to this time. Which only proved that she needed a vacation. The man was dead.

The room burst with activity. She and her sisters were responsible for uniting many of the couples present at the Valentine's Day Ball. She'd have to make sure she checked with Bridget to see how their couples were doing. Unlike the majority of matchmaking establishments, she and her sisters never lost contact with their couples and checked in on them from time to time.

She kept to the shadows as Emma and Björn were swept into the center of the room. She'd caught a glimpse of them before the crowd closed in around them. They'd looked equal parts confused and overwhelmed. It was understandable, after what they'd been through. When their lives returned to normal, they'd have questions.

She wanted to see for herself how Emma and Björn were reacting toward one another now that they'd returned. Body language and the words they spoke to each other were critical after a return.

The sisters had witnessed both extremes. The ideal outcome was where someone went down on one knee and proposed marriage. But they'd also witnessed a scenario, as in the case of their New Year's Eve event, where the couple fled from each other as soon as they'd walked through the door. She wished she could see what was going on with Emma and Björn.

Frustrated, she lifted to her tiptoes to see if she could get a better view. It was a futile attempt. She was too short. She edged along the perimeter of the crowd, looking for an opening. There was none. She whirled around, looking for something to stand on, and located a chair.

"Let me help you?" a man said.

She backed away from the chair, then froze in place. Andrew Campbell, the matchmaker council's representative, stood extending his hand. She stuffed her hands in her pockets. If history was any indication, the concept of *helping* was not in the man's skill set. On the other hand, he was very good at disrupting the order of things, destroying years of hard work, breaking hearts...

"Aren't you curious how your couple is doing?" His voice sounded like thick maple syrup. What was the man up to?

She folded her arms together. "I've changed my mind. I'll check in on them in the morning."

He looked over her head in the direction of the crowd. He'd changed from the ridiculous highwayman's costume to something that suited him more: pressed jeans, white shirt, and navy sports jacket. He had a swimmer's body, the result of years of swimming in the North Sea, near his castle in Scotland, no doubt. She resisted the impulse to ask him if he could see Emma and Björn's reactions.

He turned back toward her, staring at her with his penetrating dark eyes.

"Can you see them?" she blurted, ignoring the heat she felt under his gaze. After all this time, he still had a disturbing effect on her. She remembered her resolve not to ask him about Emma and Björn. "Never mind. They'll be fine. Emma and Björn love each other."

"Sometimes love is not enough."

He was frustratingly right, of course, and the reason the matchmaking guild and its twelve-member council were formed in the first place. The council was hereditary. When a member died, their firstborn, male or female, took their place. Andrew Campbell had just taken over after his father's death last fall.

"Love might not be enough, as you so coldly say, but neither can it be calculated by computers. A matchmaker's instincts are the best in matters of the heart. You are supposed to be a matchmaker, and yet you don't believe in soul mates or the forever-after kind of love."

Andrew looked past her as though avoiding her gaze. "You of all people should know that this is a critical time. If I were you, I'd have insinuated myself into the center of that crowd and convinced the couple that they were meant for each other. I'd remind them that they'd experienced an intense adventure, full of both romance and danger, and that they'd survived by working together. Everyday life would be a snap in comparison. If that didn't work, I'd point out that they not only got along well, but they worked out problems that came their way and discovered that they were attracted to one another. I'd explain that after what they'd experienced, marriage would be easy. When I conduct these adventures, I have a one hundred percent success rate. All my couples either get married on the spot or become at least engaged."

"The council should give you a trophy engraved with the words 'Matchmaker of the Year,' " Lady Roselyn said, injecting as much sarcasm as she could. She had a few choice words for him, and none were G-rated. "But how long do your couples stay together? That is the real test of a relationship. Our couples," she continued, "aren't numbers on a chart, they are people. My sisters and I want them to reach their own conclusions. When they return from their adventures, we do not interfere. We provide the experience. It's up to them to work out if they belong together."

"It's always about the numbers, Rose. Your old-fashioned methods are outdated, which is one of the reasons I'm here."

He turned to face her. The self-assured twinkle in his expression had been replaced with deep concern.

It felt as though her heart had stopped beating. He

hadn't called her Rose since... "What is the other reason you're here?"

"Your husband is alive. What's more, I suspect he had something to do with the trouble we had in Paris."

Lady Roselyn felt as though her legs had turned to overcooked spaghetti. "Impossible. He's dead."

"On the contrary. He's very much alive and living in France. I noticed him walking along the Seine River promenade, but when I ran after him he took off. But I swear it was him."

"I thought I saw him, as well."

Lady Roselyn felt as though she'd plunged into a glacier-fed lake. She gasped for breath and reached out for something to steady her. Then her world went dark.

Chapter Thirty-Nine

Lady Roselyn woke with a start. Someone had carried her to the Matchmaker Café's storage room and set her down on an antique velvet chaise longue. Four sets of eyes stared down at her. Two belonged to her sisters, Bridget and Fiona. They almost swooned with happiness when they realized she was still in the land of the living. The third set belonged to William, who held her hand and kept saying things like, "How are you feeling?" and "Do you want a cup of tea?"

The fourth set belonged to Andrew, whom she had decided to rename *gray-eyed-demon-sent-to-torment-me.*

"You fainted," Andrew said. "Since when do you faint?"

"Evidently, it's my new thing," she said as William helped her to a sitting position.

"I should have been there to prevent you from traveling to Paris," William said, still holding onto her hand.

She felt William's wave of protectiveness flow around her, nearly bringing her to tears. How long had she known him? Ten years? Twenty? The council called him Keeper of the Doors. A more accurate description was keeper of her heart. But the rules that barred him from love were tighter than hers.

She squeezed his hand, then slipped from his grasp.

Fiona sat down beside her. "We were all so worried about you. Are you ill?"

"It's stress," Bridget said, sitting on the other side of Lady Roselyn as she handed her a cup of tea she hadn't asked for.

Lady Roselyn stared down at the cup of steaming Earl Grey. Of late it seemed that every emotional event, for better or worse, had been marked with tea. She wasn't sure how she felt about that. Maybe she'd take a clue from Fiona and start drinking lattés.

Bridget glared at Andrew as though he was the root cause of the problem, although Lady Roselyn doubted her sister suspected the real reason. "Andrew's been bossing us around ever since he arrived," Bridget said, narrowing her gaze. "He has advice on how to match our couples, what adventures to arrange, and the type of parties we should plan. He even had the nerve to demand that Fiona and Liam stop delaying their marriage. If you ask me, when Fiona and Liam marry, or for that matter, if they decide to go their separate ways, it's none of Andrew's or the council's business."

Fiona stood to give Bridget a hug. "I love that you're defending me, but we both know the council makes the rules. We should all leave our sister alone to rest. She's earned it. This has been a long night for everyone."

Bridget gave Andrew another glare. "I'm not leaving until he does."

"Fiona's right," William said. "We still have guests to attend and a place to clean up."

Lady Roselyn watched William. Did he know?

When her sisters and William had gone, Lady Roselyn set her tea cup down on a nearby packing crate. "You didn't tell them about my husband."

"Neither did you," Andrew replied. "Are you going to tell me the real reason you fainted when you learned your husband was still alive?"

"You wouldn't believe me."

"Try me."

She started to pick up the tea again but changed her mind. "Our marriage started out as you might expect. It was an arranged marriage, like all the matchmakers in our family, but we tried to make the best of it and in the beginning we worked on developing a friendship. Then, a few months into the marriage, we decided we wanted children. When month after month came and went, and I didn't conceive, we grew further apart. We didn't make the leap to a real relationship, let alone to love, and over time even the fragile friendship we'd formed started to disintegrate. The evening of our second wedding anniversary, he said he had a solution that might help. He said he'd rented a sailboat and presented me with a folder full of romantic, tropical locations."

She rolled her neck to ease the tension, remembering the preparations before their trip. He had been so happy, so attentive, insisting that he would make all the arrangements. She let out a breath. She should have known.

"When we were out at sea," she continued, "he confessed he planned to kill me and petition the council to remarry. We fought, and the boat caught fire. The explosion blew me clear. I managed to swim to shore, but there was no trace of my husband. I assumed he'd died in the explosion."

Andrew shook his head. "That would explain the scars I saw over his hands."

Lady Roselyn pressed her hand to her mouth as her vision blurred. She squeezed her eyes shut. "Do you think he wants revenge?"

Andrew only nodded.

Chapter Forty

Lady Roselyn stuffed her hands into the pockets of her coat as she approached Emma's bakery shop. It was three o'clock in the morning, but Lady Roselyn couldn't sleep. There were too many unanswered questions, with no clear path to the answers. The best solution was to dive into work. More of her mother's wise advice.

Aside from the issue with her now-very-much-alive husband, Fiona's expression haunted her, probably because she'd recognized Fiona's struggle. Fiona had admitted she was in love with two men, knowing Lady Roselyn would understand. In her case, she'd made the wrong choice. Was that what worried Fiona? Was she afraid to make the wrong decision?

So, because she couldn't sleep, she was awake at this uncivilized time in the morning, when the majority of people were fast asleep, and she wondered if she'd lost her mind. What she was about to do went against everything in all the advice she preached to her sisters.

A light shone through a window of the bakery. Emma was still awake. Or had just awakened to start baking. After Andrew's news that her husband was alive, Lady Roselyn had to face the very real possibility that he was behind the mix-up of the doors in Paris. But why? If she was smart, she'd gather her sisters and start packing.

But something else Andrew had said also nagged at her. He believed that matchmakers had a larger role to play than just supplying an adventure and hoping things worked out with their couples. She and her sisters provided only the adventure. Although there might be a random piece of advice, now and again, they resisted the temptation to try and influence their couples.

Before she could change her mind, she knocked on the door to Emma's bakery.

It took only a matter of seconds before Emma flipped on the lights to the front of the bakery and opened the door. The look of complete disappointment that spread over the young woman's expression told Lady Roselyn she'd made the right choice. Emma had been hoping it was Björn.

Emma was still dressed in the same gown. The poor thing looked as though she had the weight of the world on her shoulders. When she just stood there, Lady Roselyn took that as her cue.

"May I come in for a little while? You look like you need someone to talk to."

Emma pulled the door wider, and Lady Roselyn walked in. The first thing she noticed was the gingerbread replica of the Debauve & Gallais Chocolate shop in Paris. A coincidence perhaps, or fate lending a helping hand? "This is a perfect reproduction."

Emma glanced toward the gingerbread house trimmed in blue and gold. "I just finished making it. My mother and I made a daily pilgrimage there during our stay. They no longer serve drinking chocolate, but there was always something new to try. We used to make a gingerbread replica of this chocolate house every year on the anniversary of our trip to Paris. But after my mother died, it was too painful. It's a funny coincidence that Björn and I were there, as well."

"I don't believe in coincidences." Lady Roselyn leaned down, noting that Emma had recreated the inside of the house to resemble the original, complete with frosted gingerbread tables and chairs. "You have a heart on the inside wall. I can't read the initials."

"My mother and I couldn't read them either. The people at the chocolate house said a legend had risen around that heart. On the eve of the French Revolution, a couple carved their names on that pillar right before escaping. Everyone who comes into the shop rubs the heart in hopes of finding good luck in romance. That's the reason the initials have faded over time. Would you like something to eat? I think I might have brownies."

"Just cocoa would be lovely," Lady Roselyn said as she followed Emma to the kitchen, watching as Emma filled a pan with milk to warm on the stove. "Call me a romantic, but I have a strong feeling that Björn carved the initials. The two of you should return and see if I'm right." Lady Roselyn's suggestion to Emma was met with only a shrug of the shoulder. "You love Björn. Why are you hesitating?"

Keeping her back turned toward Lady Roselyn, Emma switched the burner on the stove to simmer and stirred the milk. "My mother cautioned me about tying myself to the wrong man."

Lady Roselyn winced at the comment, grateful Emma's back was turned away.

Words held meaning.

She didn't know very much about Emma's parents or their relationship. What she did know was that people said things in frustration, things they didn't mean. People were stronger together, and without risk there wasn't reward.

"Do you love Björn?"

Emma took the cocoa off the burner and poured the warmed liquid into mugs, giving a nod. She gripped the counter. "More and more every day."

"Then you owe it to yourself and Björn to take a leap of faith. Your mother was well-intentioned; however, she could only speak to how she felt. Parents might shape and influence the adults we become, but how we live our lives and the people we choose to love is our decision."

"It's scary."

Lady Roselyn smiled as she accepted the cocoa. "It's also exciting."

Chapter Forty-One

Hours later, Fiona could almost feel the Matchmaker Café smile as she locked the front door. The whole world loved a happy ending. All the couples had left, the food and dishes were put away, and the musicians had been paid for a job well done. Fiona had once seen a poem in her mother's diary entitled, *A Recipe for a Successful Match.* She didn't know if her mother had written it or if the author was lost in time, but the words never seemed more appropriate than now:

Begin with a mixture of friendship,
Communication, and respect.
Add a dash of attraction.
Blend equal parts of commitment,
Trust, and honesty.
Now fold in a generous cup of love.

Fiona took in a deep breath. Had she found that forever-after kind of love with Liam? Or was she building barriers to keep him out? She laughed softly. Barriers. She and her sisters always cautioned their clients to guard against creating barriers between themselves and the people they loved. Was she guilty of the same tactic they warned others to avoid?

Whatever the case, she would have to content herself with helping others, for now. And as a bonus, she and her sisters had requests for matchmaker parties scheduled into the next year. Her instincts regarding

Emma and Björn had proven correct. They loved each other. The only question remaining was whether or not they could overcome the obstacles they'd built in the past.

But a cloud still hung over what had happened to the doors in Paris, and her sister, Lady Roselyn, was becoming more and more evasive. And what was she going to do about Liam and Duncan?

She leaned her forehead against the doorframe. So why did she feel like a leaf caught in a windstorm? She was so tired. She wanted to go someplace quiet and peaceful.

"Look what I found," Lady Roselyn announced. "You'll never guess what's inside."

Fiona shut her eyes for a moment and tried to conjure interest in the discovery. Didn't her sister ever sleep? Fiona had to find a way for the council to allow her sister to remarry. Fiona pushed away from the door, vowing to make that a priority as Lady Roselyn placed a large rectangular box on the table.

Fiona recognized the box at once. All the strength drained from her body. She reached for the window ledge nearby to keep from falling and took a calming breath. She knew exactly what was inside. It contained traditions and obligations and heartache.

Lady Roselyn untied the ribbons and lifted the lid slowly. It was as though she wanted to savor the moment when the contents would be revealed. She chatted on and on about the ball, reminiscing about happy couples and engagements.

Keeping her distance, Fiona circled the table and twisted her engagement ring. Liam had commented that he thought the ring was too loose and should be resized.

Fiona thought it was too tight. She nodded toward the box. "I thought we left that in Scotland."

Lady Roselyn shook her head as she eased back the layers of tissue. "Why on earth would we leave something this beautiful behind?"

Fiona peered into the box. Nestled on a cushion of tissue was a lace wedding gown encrusted with seed pearls. Her sister was right. It was just as she remembered. The gown was magnificent. There was also a princess-style crown, decorated with crystals and white satin rosebuds, and shoes covered in the same lace as the gown. Perhaps the wedding dress had been made this beautiful as a distraction in a situation such as hers.

Fiona folded her arms across her waist, holding herself tightly. "It won't fit."

"Nonsense. Our mother and our grandmother were exactly the same size as you are." Lady Roselyn reached in and drew it out, holding it against Fiona. The crystals caught the light and winked back at Fiona as though challenging her. "Just as I thought," Lady Roselyn continued. "The dress will fit perfectly. When you and Liam are wed, you'll make a lovely bride. We should talk about setting a date and go over the guest list. Everyone will want to attend. There hasn't been a wedding of this kind in our community in decades."

Lady Roselyn continued to talk about flowers, bridesmaids, location options, music, and food as she draped the gown over a chair and drew out the matching veil.

Fiona's pulse raced as her sister's words spun together until they blurred. Brides were supposed to look forward to their wedding day, Fiona reasoned.

They should care about the preparations and not feel as though the walls were closing in. Was this how brides felt when they faced an arranged marriage? Trapped, with no way of escape?

Liam was a fine, honorable man. His character wasn't the point. How could she know for sure that he was the one she could love for the rest of her life? Fiona reached for the edge of the table to steady her trembling.

Her gaze rested on the door that led to where she'd first met Duncan as a tear traveled a path down her cheek. She wished she and Duncan had had more time together. She wished she weren't getting married. But most of all, she wished Duncan didn't live in a castle in Scotland hundreds of years in the past. Maybe then she'd know for sure what to do.

Chapter Forty-Two

Morning sunlight streamed through Emma's window. Since dawn, she'd lain under the down comforter, alternating between listening to the sounds of the Village shopkeepers as they opened their stores and watching the light grow brighter with each passing hour. And with each hour she'd felt worse.

Waking up early was a hard habit to break, but that's not what had kept her awake. It was her conversation with Lady Roselyn.

Lady Roselyn had asked her if she loved Björn. Love was never the question. She knew that now. She'd made a mess of things. She'd asked him to give up his life as a fisherman. Why had she done that? She'd told Lady Roselyn that she was following her mother's advice. The truth was that it was her own fears that kept her closed off and Björn at a distance.

Then she'd asked her question, and when they returned, he'd disappeared. Was it too late for them?

She turned from the window. Her thoughts collided and twisted in her stomach, making it ache.

She'd ruined everything.

She threw off the covers and slid off the bed onto the icy wood floor. Her bare toes curled as she shivered and quickly slipped on her slippers and robe.

The sound of a metal pan hitting the kitchen floor below echoed toward her.

Odd. She'd given Daisy the day off.

Emma opened her bedroom door and heard the muffled sounds of conversation coming from the direction of the kitchen. She cinched the terrycloth belt tighter on her robe and hurried down the staircase that led to the kitchen. A few steps from the bottom she paused, taking in the swirl of people and activity that hummed like a well-run clock.

Mr. Rigby was shoving trays of scones into the oven, C.C. was kneading bread, Daisy was chopping walnuts and pecans, and the twins were on the floor coloring. One was dressed in a pink dress with matching leggings, and the other in an identical purple outfit. Björn was in the center, alternately directing traffic and frosting cinnamon rolls.

One of the twins looked over in Emma's direction. Her expression lit up like Christmas tree lights as she jumped to her feet. "Emma's awake."

"Good morning, sleepyhead." Björn grinned and winked.

His greeting took her breath away. She'd thought he'd never speak to her again. She loved the way his gaze captured hers and shut out the world around them. He'd always had that ability, but she'd never wanted to consider what it meant.

Emma continued down the stairs until she reached the bottom. "I don't understand. What is everyone doing here? I told everyone I'm closed today. There's a sign on the window."

Björn wiped his hands on a towel. "About that. The Village decided that they can't live without you, even for one day. Correction. *I* can't live without you," he amended. "Plus, your friends are in training for when you take time off. It takes a village, as the saying goes."

"You're a fisherman AND a philosopher. You keep surprising me."

"Or maybe our shared experience means you're finally seeing me for the first time."

Was he reading her mind? The tone of his voice wasn't judgmental. Rather, his words came as statement of fact.

"Have I always been so slow to recognize what is right in front of me?" she asked.

"I don't mind. You're worth the wait."

But she didn't want to wait any longer. She felt she was getting a second chance to get it right. She wanted to seize life with both hands and never let go. More to the point, she wanted Björn. She knew she was smiling so widely her smile must look like it covered her whole face. Björn had that effect on her. He made her laugh and smile and want to climb mountains. She wanted to shower him with kisses.

"And what is important to you, Mr. Erickson?"

"I want you by my side for as long as I live."

She loved how he talked about their future together.

Caitlin rushed over and took Emma's hand in hers. "We're all going to help you while you're gone."

"Where am I going?"

"Your honeymoon," Catherine said. "In Paris."

Emma bent toward Catherine, knowing her voice was trembling. She didn't want to read too much into the word "honeymoon." After all, the twins were very young. They might think vacations were honeymoons. "Paris is a lovely city, but I was just there."

Björn walked around the counter toward Emma.

"True, but we have to check to see if something I did is still there." His grin widened. "I carved our initials into one of the pillars in the chocolate shop."

"Like this one?" Caitlin said, pointing to the gingerbread house.

Sure enough, etched in icing were the words "Björn loves Emma" in the middle of a white icing heart.

"How did that get there…" Emma began.

Daisy came over and gathered the twins. "Björn wrote it in when you were upstairs. It's time for us to leave Emma and Björn alone, girls."

"He won't do it right if we leave him alone," Caitlin insisted.

"He has to get down on one knee," Catherine said, running over to Björn and pulling on his arm. "Did you remember the ring?"

He laughed as he knelt and pulled a red velvet box from his pocket. "It was my mother's wedding ring."

"I want to see," Caitlin said, peering around to get a closer look.

He opened the box, and inside was a heart-shaped diamond, surrounded by rubies.

Both twins ooh'ed and ah'd, then smiled over at Emma. "You're going to love it," Caitlin said. "I promise."

Emma covered her mouth with her hand to smother her laugh as her gaze met Björn's.

He shrugged and mouthed, "Sorry we're not alone."

She laughed again and mouthed the response, "It's okay."

Catherine poked Björn on the shoulder. "Ask her."

Björn looked as though he was having a difficult time keeping a straight face. "Emma…this is not how I planned it. I wanted a romantic breakfast, flowers, music. The type of proposal you deserve."

It was Caitlin's turn to nudge Björn. "You have to ask her."

"What if she says no?" her sister said.

Björn grew serious. "I can change. If you're worried about my being gone too much, I have a solution. I called Jorvy, and we talked it over. He said he'd be happy to change places with me. I want to be the person you need. Nothing matters to me if you aren't in my life."

Emma warmed under his gaze and with the words he'd spoken. He was willing to give up everything for her. She recognized the sincerity in his expression.

Her eyes blurred as she crossed the distance that separated them and caressed the side of his face with her hand. "I don't want you to give up something for me that means so much to you. You wouldn't ask that of me, and I won't of you. Fishing is part of who you are and one of the many reasons I fell in love with you. It was wrong of me to ask you to give it up." Paraphrasing from a line in the movie *Bridget Jones' Diary*, she said, "I love you just the way you are."

Caitlin nudged him and whispered again. "Ask her."

He grinned and held up the ring. "Will you marry me?"

"Yes," she said, but her answer was drowned out by the cheering of everyone in the kitchen. Even Björn's puppy got into the act, barking from the back porch as Ella let out a loud meow of approval.

Björn stood, taking Emma in his arms. "Sometimes it really does take a Village."

A word about the author…

Pam Binder is an award-winning Amazon and *New York Times* bestselling author. Pam believes in smiles, Irish and Scottish myths, and like Wonder Woman, the power of love.

Pam writes historical fiction, contemporary fiction, middle grade, and fantasy.

Visit her at:

http://pambinder.com

Thank you for purchasing
this publication of The Wild Rose Press, Inc.

If you enjoyed the story, we would appreciate your
letting others know by leaving a review.

For other wonderful stories,
please visit our on-line bookstore at
www.thewildrosepress.com.

For questions or more information
contact us at
info@thewildrosepress.com.

The Wild Rose Press, Inc.
www.thewildrosepress.com

Stay current with The Wild Rose Press, Inc.

Like us on Facebook

https://www.facebook.com/TheWildRosePress

And Follow us on Twitter
https://twitter.com/WildRosePress